She held the call button down and yelled.

"Ranger station? Anyone? Help! This is naturalist Tamala Roth. Clint and I are being chased by another car on the road about a quarter mile beyond the overpass. Send backup to Grand Loop. Now!"

The Hummer slammed into them and jerked the truck forward, jarring Tamala's neck. They skidded to a stop on the side of the road.

Tamala heard herself scream as she saw Clint's forehead hit the steering wheel. Her own tight seat belt kept her in place, but the jolt left her woozy. The Hummer's door creaked open then slammed shut close by.

She locked the passenger's side door. Clint groaned next to her, his head still on the steering wheel, but he didn't move.

The driver's side door opened and a huge man yanked Clint out of his seat and let him fall to the ground. The man's voice was a low, rumbling rasp. "He won't be helping you this time. You'll pay for taking my chance at that bear and for seeing my face."

Kari Trumbo is an internationally bestselling author of historical and contemporary Christian romance and romantic suspense. She loves reading, listening to contemporary Christian music, singing when no one's listening and curling up near the woodstove when winter hits. She makes her home in central Minnesota—where the trees and lakes are plentiful—with her husband of over twenty years, two daughters, two sons, a few cats and a bunny who's the star of one of her books.

Books by Kari Trumbo

Love Inspired Suspense

Deadly Yellowstone Secrets

Visit the Author Profile page at LoveInspired.com.

DEADLY YELLOWSTONE SECRETS

KARI TRUMBO

LOVE INSPIRED SUSPENSE
INSPIRATIONAL ROMANCE

LOVE INSPIRED® SUSPENSE
INSPIRATIONAL ROMANCE

Recycling programs
for this product may
not exist in your area.

ISBN-13: 978-1-335-59773-1

Deadly Yellowstone Secrets

For questions and comments about the quality of this book, please contact us
at CustomerService@Harlequin.com.

Love Inspired
22 Adelaide St. West, 41st Floor
Toronto, Ontario M5H 4E3, Canada
www.LoveInspired.com

Printed in U.S.A.

Be strong and of a good courage, fear not, nor be afraid of them: for the Lord thy God, he it is that doth go with thee; he will not fail thee, nor forsake thee.
—*Deuteronomy* 31:6

I dedicate this book to Rich and Peggy Henderson, for their love and knowledge of Yellowstone National Park. I wouldn't have been able to write this book without them.

ONE

The growing darkness didn't make Tamala Roth's hike easy, but the nip in the November air cooled her heated skin. Bears were notoriously active at dawn and dusk and she only had a few more minutes to gather her data. Scrub grass clung to her socks as she picked up a discarded candy wrapper then continued on the trail. The path led from the Kepler Cascades toward home in the Old Faithful area.

Tracking bears as they headed for their dens for their winter sleep was getting more and more difficult. They'd fattened up over the last few weeks, but would soon hole up in their dens until warmer weather arrived. This would be one of her last chances to document the particular mama bear she loved the most. But she'd yet to see the famous bear that evening.

A rifle blast stopped her in her tracks.

Her heart raced as she reached for her walkie. Mama, the black bear she'd tracked for months, raced from a wooded area about forty yards from where she stood, moving along the line of trees. Tamala held still. If she ran, any bear moving like that might chase her. The bear slowed, glancing back and forth. *Run!* She wasn't sure if she meant Mama, her or both of them.

She held her breath, waiting, keeping still to avoid being seen. Mama stood and craned her neck back and forth, then ducked back into the trees along a used bear path farther from where she'd emerged. She focused all her attention on the bear to recall every detail.

A man in camouflage appeared from the woods, raising his rifle to his shoulder, aiming at where Mama had just disappeared. Tamala screamed and dropped to the ground, covering her head as he swiveled the barrel toward her. She held in a cry as a second shot rent the air.

Through the blades of tall grass, she watched him hunt. Was he looking for the bear, or her? Poachers hunted the area. No matter how hard she worked to give information to the rangers, rarely did they catch poachers. Her naturalist team speculated someone on the inside might be at fault. The prevalence of the poachers and the timing of their hunts made it seem like only someone who knew the rangers could get away with so much.

She stretched out her neck to see above the grass, thankful she'd forgotten her bright hiking vest. The man yanked the bolt on his rifle, ejecting the casing, and loaded the next round. He seemed oddly familiar. Moving steadily toward her, he pulled the rifle to his shoulder, swinging the barrel back and forth, his eye looking down the sight.

She needed to get away somehow without alerting him to her location hidden in the grass. Stretching back, she felt around in her pocket. She had her walkie in hand, but its use was loud. Her phone would be silent if she could reach it. The Velcro closure securing her phone slowed her down, but if she could reach it, she could call for help.

She took in all his distinguishing features. Hair, brown. Face, angry. Jaw, angular. Muscular build, but lean. About six foot or a little taller. She slid her finger along her pocket flap, slowly releasing the tape, trying to open the closure without a sound. Sweat beaded over her face as she both hurried and took care. He drew closer, about thirty yards from her now. She forced her breathing to slow as she'd learned in bear training. If she was calm, she could think.

Examining him too closely might bring her to his attention. Her hand slipped and the Velcro tore loudly, sending a distant bird to flight. She halted as the poacher spun and their eyes locked. Seconds seemed to slow, and she memorized his face.

A moment later, he had a bead on her, carefully sweeping the muzzle like a professional. She leaped up and ran, but the woods were behind her. Nothing but grass and the well-trodden ground of the path lay before her. The road might be close enough, but that offered no protection.

Feet pounding to get away, she heard a shot and braced for impact as her knees hit the ground. She folded into a ball and rolled, hearing his feet crunch in the dirt right behind her. Staggering back up, she raced for the trees, hoping that the lack of pain meant he hadn't hit her.

She prayed one of the law enforcement rangers was nearby and had heard the shots. They were the protectors of the National Park System, like a police force. They were her only chance at making it out of this alive.

Clint Jackson, the law enforcement ranger over the Old Faithful area, pulled to a stop on the service road and climbed out of his truck. She'd never been so happy to see anyone. "Clint!" She tried to both wave and run. Rapid footfalls approaching reminded her she wasn't out of the woods yet.

Behind her, the poacher ran for cover. He pulled a handgun from his holster and wildly aimed at her. She launched to the ground and the thud of the bullet hit near her. Now she knew what the bear felt like. Hunted for sport.

Clint raised his service pistol, and she covered her head, afraid to be in the way. Clint could end this. She waited for the shot, or at least for a verbal warning. That poacher had been aiming at her. Clint was within the law to shoot. Why didn't he?

She raised her head then chanced a look over her shoulder. The poacher was gone. She stood and brushed herself off, then went to meet the ranger. "Clint…why didn't you shoot?" She hoped he wouldn't see how badly she shook.

He took a moment to look her over, then his steely eyes met hers. "I saw a guy aiming his gun at you near the trees, but he was too far away for me to get an accurate shot, especially with you there. We're too close to the road and I didn't have a good line of sight. I don't think it's a good idea to chase an armed suspect in the dark, alone. We'll get your statement and try to catch up with him in the morning. The gates are closing. I'm sorry." He briefly touched her arm.

The contact was meant to be apologetic, but her heart ratcheted at the brief contact. "Clint, he's a poacher. It's not like he cares about opening and closing rules. He saw me when I accidentally made too much noise. He took a shot at me… He's seen me. This park is massive, over three thousand square miles in three states. He could be anywhere." She had a right to be worried about this.

He nodded, and something in his demeanor told her he wanted her to stay nearby. Since she had no idea where the poacher went, she'd listen. He reached for the walkie on his shoulder. "Attempted poaching and murder. About two miles south toward Kepler." He waved for her to come along with him. They approached the area where the poacher had been and he kneeled next to the spent shell casing from the poacher's gun. "Which bear?"

"Mama," she answered. The bear was known for having twins and for being a fiercely protective mother.

His face shifted from handsome to stony. "She's been in Yellowstone awhile. She's one of our most popular. My team will need to get in here and look over her path, see if that poacher got any of her cubs."

She agreed. As a naturalist, the law enforcement team didn't need her help for that, especially since seeing Mama today had been an accident. She had been looking for Mama, but following another bear when Mama had run from the woods. "Where did the shooter go?" She stood on her toes and searched for any sign of the poacher. Exhaustion tugged on her to sit and rest, but she refused to give in.

Clint pulled an evidence bag from his thigh pocket,

turned it inside out, then picked up the casing. "Not sure, but I let my team know there's a poacher on the loose and told them to watch the exits for anything suspicious." Turning from her, he mumbled something else into his walkie. He glanced at her, and his eyes softened. Protectively, he laid a hand on her shoulder. "Hey, you've been through a lot. Why don't you sit for a minute and just take some deep breaths, okay?"

Her mouth went dry for a moment. She'd been told by other naturalists not to trust the law enforcement team when it came to poaching, but she wanted to trust Clint. She shook the strange sensation from her arm. "I'll be fine. I just want to catch this guy. He took a shot at Mama and me. I want to see him arrested."

While he searched around the area for other evidence, she moved off to the side and did as he suggested. Her chest hurt from her pounding heart. Poaching wasn't new, but seeing a gun pointed at her firsthand left a deep mark on her.

After calming herself, she joined Clint in the search for other clues. "I don't understand how you saw him close enough to see him aim at me, but not be close enough to do something."

No one ever seemed to catch these guys. They moved around like they were invincible, which was another reason her team suspected at least one ranger might be in on it. Unless the reason Clint had done nothing was because he knew the poacher…

He cocked his head slightly before he replied, "It wasn't a clear shot. I saw you in the open and him through a break in the tree cover as he ran. I'd come this way because I heard the first shot at the bear from where I was at Kepler."

His reasons made sense, but still didn't explain everything, like why he didn't just jump in his truck and follow him. She'd heard the whispered rumors for as long as she'd worked in the park that the poaching started from Yellowstone's very own rangers. No one wanted to believe the talk, but why else let the guy go?

"And you called in for help, right? We might catch him before he leaves the park." People didn't just disappear, or she would've done just that when she'd run from the poacher.

He took a deep breath and pointed near a bend in the road. "I didn't take chase right away because people were heading to the exits. What if there had been a car I didn't see coming around that bend? I might have accidentally shot a civilian. I also wanted to make sure you were safe. If I had given chase and left you alone, he could have circled back and shot at you again. Speaking of which." He reached for her wrist and did a pulse check, causing her to catch her breath. Why did his touch make her heart race? She should be furious with him.

"Are you hurt in any way?"

She'd never had much reason to talk to the handsome ranger, but having his attention now stirred emotions in her she'd buried for years. She slowly met his gaze and shook her head. "I'm fine. Just shaken up a bit."

As the law enforcement ranger, he was the closest thing to a nurse available as the rangers made everything ready to close the park to summer visitors. Within weeks, that poacher would've been able to sneak onto national land and do his business with no one the wiser until much too late.

A truck rumbled down the road, carrying two wildlife rangers. They got out and pulled heavy backpacks over their shoulders from the rear of the truck. Clint waved them over, and Tamala stood back to let him talk to his team.

Yellowstone suddenly didn't feel like home. The land with its huge mountain vistas and wide-open sky had always fit her. From the moment she'd stepped foot in the park, she'd wanted to live there. For all but about two months of the year, when the park service required her to leave for the season, she did.

As a naturalist and tour guide in Yellowstone, she got to enjoy the park she loved by giving informational tours, classes for visitors, and—her specialty—studying the bears. During the winter season, when the park was partially open, they didn't need naturalists and concessioners. Only a few full-year rangers, including Clint, stayed. He turned to face her, and his deep blue eyes caught her gaze.

"I'm not okay with letting you walk back alone after you saw that guy's face. Even if you didn't get a picture, you might be able to pick him out from a crowd. He aimed a gun at you, and I need to be sure you get home safely. My truck is warm and waiting. Why don't you go sit in there? I'll be over shortly."

She headed to the pickup without argument, especially since the mental shock of what happened had kicked in and she had a case of the shakes like never before. After closing herself in the pickup's warmth, she noted Clint's map. He'd just been at the falls.

Her mind raced for a moment, recalling all she'd seen. She'd been in the same area, but he hadn't been there that she saw. Yellowstone National Park encompassed 56 miles from end to end, 3472 square miles, and 142 miles of the Grand Loop Road, enough ground that she may have missed seeing him, unless he wasn't really there.

If Clint was working with the poachers, he wasn't about to shoot one of them. He hadn't even yelled to get the poacher's attention. The truck suddenly felt like the last place she wanted to be, especially since Clint carried a gun. She was smarter than to put herself right in the poacher's bull's-eye twice in one day if Clint was more sinister than he'd seemed. "I think I'll be fine walking," she mumbled aloud to herself.

She climbed out of the pickup just as Clint approached. She hated that the hair on her arms prickled to life as he looked at her. Was he eyeing her up like the poacher had? Yet the appreciative look in his eyes said he was sizing her up in a very different way from her enemy.

A few days before, Yellowstone Search and Rescue had finished a winter training exercise. They'd trekked Craig Pass by Lone Star Geyser, a popular ski trail for winter visitors and nearly the same terrain they would drive through. Sometimes, they needed to use GPS to find missing "persons," training dummies used for searches. Even experts with trained dogs had trouble finding them in a park full of natural elements made for obliterating someone's scent. Riding into a situation where she might never be seen again was too foolish to consider.

Ahead of her, something swooped down in a jagged zigzag pattern in the twilight. The snap of a twig to her right stopped her cold. Unease crackled in the air and up her spine. *It's a bat, Tamala...* She reminded herself these were naturally occurring noises. Not everything was the return of the armed man.

In the distance, an engine blasted to life and gunned away from them, leaving silence behind other than the rangers' muffled voices as they took notes a few feet away.

"If that's him, he'll be long gone by the time we find his tire tracks." Clint crossed his arms, stretching his green ranger uniform taught across his chest.

"Where's your coat?" she asked. The question might be silly, but if he'd been out by the falls, where the spray chilled skin enough to hurt, then his lack of coat made even less sense. It hadn't been in his truck that she recalled.

"It's in the bed of my truck. Why don't you climb back in?"

He seemed suddenly hesitant, like he wasn't sure what her holdup might be, but didn't want to give her a direct order.

"I'm sure I'll be fine. I'll text you when I get home."

"Do you have a vehicle nearby?" The question stopped her. He wasn't forcing her to get in, but questioning her safety. She'd always known him to be a respected ranger to the Park Service. In matters of safety, he was *the* man to call. Could she be mistaken? He glanced at the sky, skepticism in his handsome furrowed brow.

In Yellowstone, that look was the unspoken worry

of how quickly the sun set in the winter. And how fast the temperature dropped. "I hiked. I don't have an easy way home."

He came close and opened the door to his truck, indicating she should get in. Clint wasn't her direct supervisor, but everyone had to follow the law enforcement rangers in each of the more than ten separate areas.

Clutching her phone just in case, she climbed back into the seat she'd just left and shrugged out of her backpack, laying it at her feet.

"I'll give you a ride to your barracks to make sure you get there safely. If you hear or see anything tonight, I want you to let me know immediately." There was the order she was expecting, yet her chest loosened some instead of tightening. He was doing what a law enforcement ranger would do, not a poacher. The scientist in her looked at what she knew to be true and what she'd heard, then weighed the differences. She'd have to trust Clint, at least tentatively for now. Until he gave her a concrete reason not to.

She gave him a slight salute and settled into the passenger seat. She'd known Clint as a ranger for three years, but had never worked closely with him. He kept to himself, as did the men under him.

As he traveled north, he slowly made his way through a few turns toward the Old Faithful Inn. The tall, grand old building sat nestled in the trees, as amazing to Tamala as its namesake. Known as the largest log structure in the world, it was a good enough reason alone to visit the park.

A large black Hummer jerked out onto the road after them. The truck followed as Clint turned down the service road leading behind the Old Faithful Inn. Though Clint didn't appear nervous, his eyes darted from the rearview mirror to the side mirror and back again.

The barely used way was a shortcut to the main road. There was no reason that truck should be there. He should've been heading for the exit. She turned in her seat to see if the driver was the poacher. He seemed tall enough to be. No other passengers sat in the front.

Her instinct told her to run. Get away. The Hummer aggressively pulled closer to them and revved its engine. She glanced at Clint. His shoulders tensed and his gaze tracked from the road to his mirrors constantly.

He pressed the button on his shoulder walkie. "Command Center, this is LER Jackson." He rattled off some numbers that mixed in her head as she tried to control her shaking. Only a crackly reply came through.

Clint turned onto Grand Loop Road as fast as he dared, sending Tamala sliding across her seat and into the door. She held tight to the handle, her nerves on high alert. The only option was to go straight on the two-lane road and pray the Hummer didn't follow. The poacher immediately turned in right behind them, almost hitting their bumper.

"Clint?" She wasn't sure what else to ask. He obviously saw the guy and knew the danger.

"The safest place to go is the employee housing area, but I don't want him to know where you live. You know as well as I do options are few."

Lord, where do we go? Her chest thrummed as she searched for a way out.

The Hummer gunned its engine and cut them off, preventing an escape by dodging into the lane over the interchange and toward home. Tamala gripped the door as Clint took the off ramp heading west away from the Old Faithful area. Out into the park and too much solitude.

"We know the area better than he does. We'll lose him." He gripped the steering wheel and pushed his truck faster. "Call in backup." He tipped his head toward his shoulder.

She could describe the man in the Hummer if they got away. No vehicles had driven past. The park had closed for the night, meaning they were alone.

With the walkie silent, she reached over and took it from his shoulder, then held the call button down and yelled. "Ranger station? Anyone? Help! This is naturalist Tamala Roth. Clint and I are being chased by another car on the road about a quarter mile beyond the overpass. Do you read?"

She heard the fear in her own voice and hoped she hadn't garbled the message. The walkies could be ineffective. She waited for a noise, anything, to show someone knew where they were.

"LER Clint? This is command. Over." the voice crackled at them.

Tamala pressed the button. "Yes, send backup to Grand Loop. Now!"

"He keeps gunning his engine, then backing off. Pretty soon, we'll be in the middle of nowhere." Clint glanced in the rearview as the Hummer slammed into them and jerked the truck forward, jarring Tamala's neck and deploying Clint's airbag. They skidded to a stop on the side of the road.

Tamala heard herself scream as blood smeared on Clint's nose where the airbag hit him. Her own tight seat belt kept her in place, but the jolt left her woozy. She refused to look behind, but the SUV's door creaked open then slammed shut close by.

She locked the passenger's side door. Clint groaned next to her, his head still on the steering wheel, but he didn't move. The driver's side door opened and a huge man yanked Clint out of his seat and let him fall to the ground.

His voice was a low, rumbling rasp. "He won't be helping you this time. You'll pay for taking my chance at that bear and for seeing my face."

He wore a dark skullcap and thick coat, hiding whatever shape his body might be other than large. Beady eyes locked with hers. The threat in them was clear. There was no question. He was the man who shot at her and the bear.

She licked her dry lips and prayed her voice didn't quiver. "They'll find you. You won't get away with this." Words came easily, but not the know-how to defend herself.

He leaned forward and his chilly stare sent an unwelcome shiver down her back. "You won't have to worry your pretty little head about those bears no more."

In under a month, mid-December, she was supposed to be on a plane back to her family home in Florida for winter break for a couple months. There, she'd spend her time going over all the data she'd collected about the bears in Yellowstone. She'd submitted a grant proposal to study them all year, but the government hadn't been quick to respond. Now she wondered if she'd ever get the chance.

He made a grab for her wrist and yanked, surprising her out of her fevered thoughts. She gripped the door handle with her other hand to stay put, but he slowly dragged her toward the open driver's side door. In a fit of self-preservation, she pulled her knee to her chest and kicked. Her muscular legs from daily tours were her greatest defense.

The steely black glint of a weapon on his belt caught her eye in the dim light of dusk. Her foot connected with her attacker's arm, keeping him from grabbing her again.

"Let me go!" She freed her wrist from his iron grip and slid back to the opposite side of the cab, plastering herself to the passenger door for protection. If he wanted her, he'd have to climb all the way in and then she'd duck out the other way. She wouldn't go down without a fight.

The man narrowed his eyes as he leaned into the cab of Clint's truck, resting his knee against the seat. "You want to do this the hard way?" He reached for his belt and drew a gun, then slowly racked the slide, pulling the top of the gun back to engage the bullet. The *click* filled her ears in the still, cold night.

Her pulse raced as she flattened herself against the door of the pickup. The roar of a big truck sounded as lights came to a stop on Grand Loop Road. One of Clint's men jumped out. From where they were down in the ditch, he seemed a mile away. Her attacker stuffed the gun back into his belt and squinted at the coming assistance.

"You're going to jail where you belong." Though she didn't know for sure. Doubt still held her captive.

He'd managed to escape before, impossible as that scenario seemed. The poacher leaned in the truck, reaching for her. She screamed and punched out at him as he grabbed the dangling stuffed bear she kept hanging from the zipper on her backpack. Her fist connected with his cheek.

He flinched as he backed out of the cab. "This isn't over. Not by a long shot." He stuffed the bear into his pocket and cocked the pistol, then raised it, leveling the weapon at the man racing toward them.

Her blood pulsed in her temples as she realized if she did nothing, a man would die. With a scream, she lunged across the seat, pushing her attacker to the ground.

"Freeze!" Mark, Clint's second in command skidded to a stop, his pistol at the ready.

Tamala scrambled to get away from the poacher. "He's got a gun!" she screamed.

The poacher took a shot at Mark as he ran toward his truck, almost invisible in the dark. Without a backward glance, he took off in his Hummer. Breathing a sigh of relief as the poacher disappeared, Tamala kneeled at Clint's side to check on him.

She felt all around his head, gingerly examining his bloody nose where the airbag had caught him. "Over here!" she called to Mark, who'd climbed back into his truck to take chase. Clint was more important.

Clint's pounding head woke him, and he quickly realized he was now on the cold ground beside the truck.

He groped for something solid to hold on to and found someone's knee.

"It's okay. Mark's here," said a soft voice that definitely wasn't Mark. He opened his eyes to find Tamala Roth's concerned face hovering over him. He'd gone through a gamut of emotions that afternoon, from worry to much more, concerning this one woman.

"How...?" Where had he been going and why? Tamala wasn't on his team. He rarely met up with the naturalists.

"They ran us off the road. A poacher."

He closed his eyes and tried to pull all his memories from the day into order as someone else kneeled next to him. "You all right?" Mark probed Clint's face, near his tender nose.

"I will be as soon as we catch this guy." As the fogginess in his mind dissipated, he remembered the shots, the bear, a man aiming a gun at Tamala and driving her home to keep her safe. That last part hadn't worked out. He rubbed his head gingerly.

"Anyone get any information on the truck?" He glanced to Tamala, realizing for the first time she had to be close to his age and her chocolate brown hair was pretty when it was free from her usual ponytail.

She flinched slightly and frowned. "Sorry. Anything beyond self-preservation flew right out of my head. All I could think about was that I would not live long enough to enjoy the winter season or see another bear cub again."

Mark took a minute to check Clint's pupils with a small flashlight and his pulse. He did the same for Tamala.

Clint stood carefully and leaned against the truck for

support until his head stopped swimming. He took a moment to find his voice. "I'll want to check you over again in the morning when you come in to fill out a report about this. I want to make sure you didn't get whiplash."

From the little he knew of her personally, she was smart and fiercely independent, even if she didn't seem so to others with her petite size. His scrutiny would annoy her, but rules had to be followed. He had to keep a close eye on her to be certain she hadn't been hurt.

She shook her head and glanced away again. "I'll be fine, Clint. Nothing to worry about. No sense in making more work than we need. I don't want to hassle you."

"It's not a hassle, and a report is required." He rubbed his head, wondering how to drive back to the Old Faithful area with his brain so foggy.

Mark put away his flashlight and grabbed a pen, clicking it a few times. He wrote something down on a small pad of paper. "I don't have anything on the guy or the truck. At least he didn't hit you all the way into the pines. There aren't even tire tracks to follow with the pavement."

"He stole my stuffed bear." Tamala's voice shook a little, and Clint turned his focus completely on her.

"Your bear? Why?" He'd shot at a real bear, then taken a stuffed one? What was the connection?

"He almost seemed to know it meant a lot to me." She shivered. "And he knows the park. Well, enough that he got away earlier without either of us knowing where he'd gone."

With Clint leaning heavily against his truck, Tamala asked to drive. Clint handed over the keys reluctantly.

He waved to Mark as he settled into the passenger seat. "I want you to get us to your door, then I'll drive to my place on my own. I don't want you walking alone tonight. Maybe not at all until we catch this guy. Threats and poaching are one thing, but whoever this guy is, he has it out for you."

He had to give her credit. She didn't huddle in the corner. She still looked awake and alert, ready in case anyone came upon them again.

"He might, but he went after you, too."

The poacher wouldn't know Clint hadn't seen him. He'd seen the color of the man's hair and little else. When the poacher had raised his gun, Clint's heart had fallen through his feet when he saw someone he recognized as the actual target—Tamala.

If he'd taken a shot at the poacher and hit Tamala, he'd rightfully lose his badge.

"Yeah, but I've got protection. You don't." Though he'd do his best to provide what he could once she came in and told him exactly what she knew. The Yellowstone naturalists denied the rumors of poachers within their ranks, but he'd wondered how outsiders slipped in without the help of someone on the inside.

Maybe Tamala needed to be watched more than she needed someone watching out for her.

TWO

After convincing Clint she would be fine driving the short distance home from the naturalist station where her truck was parked near his house, she delivered him home. Tamala got her old yellow truck from employee parking and drove carefully as it grumbled over a few speed bumps on the way to her small cabin. Her home sat at the end of a row of six houses, all alike, painted dark brown.

She didn't need much room, nor did she care about the old age of the dwellings. Her cabin was where she kept her notes, studies and dreams for her future with Yellowstone Park.

She passed rows of empty RV spots, bare after a long summer. During the warm months, they filled those spaces like sardines with seasonal concession workers who didn't live in the dorms or bungalows. Even some seasonal rangers lived in them. Now, this late in the year, most had gone. Only three or four spots stayed occupied. Other cars parked down the row of houses, in exactly the order they should be. People were just as much creatures of habit as the animals she studied.

Jitters from the last few hours made her cautious as she gathered her bag and glanced around for anything she might have missed. Nothing seemed out of the ordinary, but that didn't stop her nerves from sending prickles up her arms and down her spine.

She grabbed her walkie and locked the truck. A last long glance confirmed no one lingered nearby. The door wasn't far, and she kept her eyes open for anything. The poacher couldn't possibly know where she lived, could he?

With the turn of her front door key, she felt safe again. Once inside, she opened her laptop and turned on her cell phone hot spot. Mama, the bear the poacher had targeted, was one of her personal favorites. She would have been gravely missed and Tamala said a quick prayer of thanks that the bear had lived through the day, and that she had, too.

The following afternoon, fellow naturalist Meghan Dale knocked briefly. "Tam? You in there?"

As much as Tamala wanted to bask in a little quiet after the previous long day, talking to a friend might help. She quickly answered the door and let her inside.

"I heard what happened. You okay?" Meghan gave her a quick hug and headed for the fridge. She brushed her dark hair behind her ear as she peered inside. "Girl, you've got no comfort food. How can you relax without some cocoa or chicken noodle soup?"

She hadn't shopped recently, since she'd have to leave the park soon. "I'll make something. Don't worry about me."

Meghan ignored her and pulled some lunch meat and

cheese from the fridge, then bread from the cupboard and started making a melt on the stove. "This whole thing must be unnerving."

She hadn't even realized the news had gotten around to the naturalists yet. "Getting chased and run off the road by a poacher is a pretty big deal." Tamala wasn't sure what else she could say, nor was she sure what Meghan had heard.

Meghan flipped the sandwich with practiced ease. "I don't know that I could've held up under the pressure."

"I *didn't*," Tamala corrected. "Clint did. At least through most of it." Just thinking about his calm presence helped soothe her nerves more. Until she reminded herself that he could just as easily be involved.

"Clint was with you?" Meghan narrowed her eyes. "That's surprising. I didn't know you two worked together."

"We don't." Why did the question feel invasive? She didn't want to talk about Clint with Meghan. "He happened to be close by when the poacher attacked and it's his job."

Her friend ignored her. "That's still odd. He rarely patrols that way." She tapped her chin. "I know you normally can't leave a mystery alone, but I hope you're not considering trying to figure out who this poacher is. If he went after you, you should request to go home."

That probably would be the smart thing to do, but would the park service allow her to leave early? If she did, would the poacher follow?

"I don't plan to go hunting for him, but Clint was going to look into finding him today. He needs me to give a statement about what the poacher looked like."

Which reminded her she was supposed to go back to the ranger station to file the report. She'd hesitated writing it out. Filing it would leave a trail if anyone did anything to her. If the poacher was working with someone right in his office, they would know exactly how much she knew—and didn't—about the man who'd tried to kill her.

"Wait, you saw him?" Meghan's voice dropped to a whisper. "Like, his face?" Her concern seemed odd, given the many other things she could worry about.

"I didn't see him well enough to definitely ID him." Meghan's strange concern made her hold in the little she knew. The trouble was, he'd seen her face as well. He might find her if he looked hard enough. She'd be an easy target.

"He's a poacher. After animals. Which means I'm in no danger, but the bears are," Tamala spoke the words to calm her own heart more than anything else and hoped Meghan hadn't heard about how he'd chased down Clint's truck. "I hope they catch him for the sake of the park. He was after Mama."

Meghan snorted then slid the sandwich on a plate and set it in front of Tamala. "Most poachers are cowards, I think. But they are stealthy. You'd better stay with other people until this all gets sorted out."

"Sorted out? You think I'm in danger?" How much did everyone know? Why would she have to stay around other people? She worked alone most of the time. Without Clint, she had no help to get out of the park or anywhere else.

"I'm sure he'll leave." Meghan flopped onto a chair. "I wish we had pizza delivery in the park."

Yellowstone offered a once in a lifetime opportunity, but working there did have downsides, like no delivery pizza. "I think I have a frozen pepperoni in the back of the freezer. Or…" She handed half her sandwich to Meghan.

"Frozen is not the same as melty, gooey delivery. I can never afford the nicer ones." She turned down the sandwich with a wave.

"Do you need a seasonal job?" Tamala had considered temporary work, too, but her pay was sufficient that she'd never sought anything else. Her family loved to have her home in Florida.

"Yeah. Never mind me. Only whining. How are you going to avoid this poacher?" Meghan went on.

Tamala closed her eyes and wished Meghan would forget about him. She tried to think of all the places she could hide within and outside of Yellowstone. The only place she could think of was Florida, but what if trouble followed her? Then her family would be in danger.

Clint's face appeared in her mind for a second as she remembered his warnings, but she brushed the thought away as quickly. He lived and worked in Yellowstone all winter. Wives and their children were allowed to live on-site with full-time rangers, but she wasn't either of those things. The park service forbade anyone else from staying during the closed winter season. They certainly wouldn't allow her to hunker down in the park because she was afraid to leave.

She bent her head to relieve the tension in her neck. "I shouldn't have to. When has a poacher ever gone after a person?" She tried to laugh, but couldn't quite manage the task in the face of the truth.

"He saw your face. You could convict him. What if he's a big poacher here in Yellowstone?" Meghan cocked her head. "You shouldn't ignore this." Her hazel eyes accused Tamala of letting go too quickly.

Flashes from earlier popped through her mind, the most prevalent being the poacher raising his gun at her face. There were various places to hide secretly in the park for the Yellowstone winter season. Living in them wouldn't be easy, because there was no heat and she'd be in survival mode, but there were options. Some rangers lived in remote cabins that were difficult to get to or find. They stayed for months at a time. That much privacy would provide the perfect off-grid hiding spot.

"I'm not ignoring any of it. My options are few. I have nowhere to go. People I love would be in danger if he's really after me."

"Go to the park service and ask for help. You need to go now. This is huge and dangerous."

The silence in the room only seemed to amplify Meghan's words.

"How do you know?" Threats were only words until someone took action. She had to believe that. Was Meghan afraid this might bring trouble to her as well?

"I just feel it. Take this seriously and go."

Clint parked his pickup in front of the ranger station and walked next door to the small medical office. Nearby, there was a visitor center, the Old Faithful Inn, the Snow Lodge, some camping cabins, gift shops, gas stations and a post office. All existed to attract park visitors to relax and spend time and money.

The temporary medical staff had locked up the small

clinic for the season, leaving him as the only means of first aid. He checked to make sure they had supplies after the attack on Tamala. After the truck hit them from behind, the scene blurred in his memory until he'd woken up on the ground with her by his side.

Assaults were fairly rare in Yellowstone. Even animal attacks on visitors, statistically, were uncommon. People who wanted to hurt his workers were unwelcome; he'd escort them out of the park himself. First he had to know what or who had attacked. Tamala hadn't made her report yet. If she wasn't willing to talk to him in his office, she might feel more comfortable conversing in her own home. He would head over there next.

Part of him really looked forward to seeing her again. He went over what he knew in his mind, but fact and rumor were two different things and her fear the day before had been genuine. If she was in league with the poacher, she'd certainly done a good job of acting afraid.

She'd also defended herself, him and Mark. That had to count for something. That had to be why he kept glancing at his watch and feeling like the day wasn't going fast enough. He'd hoped she would stop in to see him, but she hadn't come by yet.

Once he reached her bungalow, he parked his truck and got out.

He pressed the button on his walkie. "Any updates on the missing Hummer?" He waited for a reply.

"Recorded footage of a dark Hummer matching your description leaving the park last night. Still waiting on video enhancement to see if we can identify the driver. Over."

He resisted frustration. The video team was excellent, but the quality of the people didn't always mean the technology would give them what they needed. He wanted Tamala out of the park before she got hurt.

Static broke the silence, and Tamala's voice crackled over the airwaves. "Sorry, sir. I meant to come find you. I went back to my cabin to get something and lost track of time."

Hopefully, her forgetfulness didn't mean she had a concussion. At least she'd checked in. The only issue was, dark Hummers were everywhere and without the plate number, that truck could've come right back in that morning. Meaning Tamala was still in danger.

When he reached her door, he heard muffled talking inside.

"Clint is looking for me. What should I do?"

Another woman answered, "You should get him to sign a waiver for you so you can leave. Then you should get in your old pickup and get out of here."

That sounded like Meghan, another naturalist in the park. Why was she adding stress to the situation? He'd been on duty all day and hadn't seen the Hummer. He knocked and listened closely. Inside, he heard the sharp sounds of a chair scraping across the floor, then footsteps. The door opened and Tamala's eyes widened. "Clint? I didn't expect you to come all the way over. Is something wrong?" She glanced around him, her eyes flitting all over.

Wrong? Only that she seemed more terrified now than she had last evening during the incident, and she'd disregarded a direct order to follow up with him. "Have you seen anything suspicious since yesterday?" There was no way to protect her in a park this big if she didn't keep in touch and talk to him.

Her eyes widened as she glanced between him and back at Meghan. A battle warred behind her eyes, but what wasn't she telling him? Her pupils dilated quickly, and he had the sudden urge to apologize for being abrupt.

She shook her head slightly. "I'm sorry. I came back here and went to bed last night, then I was doing tours all day." She gave an apologetic look. "I meant to text you, but it slipped my mind. I didn't mean to ignore your order."

"Are you sore, hurt?" He watched for signs she was hiding any pain. A spark passed between them as her eyes registered his concern.

She rubbed the back of her neck. "Not yet. I don't think he hit us too hard."

The Hummer was a rental. He'd noticed the insignia the night before, so that might lead to something, but he'd never seen a poacher want to harm anyone—any *human*, that is. They usually just found somewhere else to poach. "Do you know who this guy is? I might understand a little road rage in our park since the speed limits are so low... But running us off the road? People don't do that without motive. Could this be an old boyfriend, a coworker? Did he recognize you when you saw him?" His stomach twisted at the thought of either.

She shook her head. "No, I don't *think* I know him." She blinked a few times and glanced away. "I've never seen that vehicle before yesterday, but his face seemed almost familiar. There's nothing I can tell you that you didn't see yourself."

Her defensive posture warned him she wasn't telling him the full story or something more bothered her than she would share. She might not be lying, but it seemed she knew more than she'd said. "Why do I get the feeling there's more to this story?"

Meghan chose that moment to speak up. She stood quickly and glared at him. "Why should she trust you? Every time there's a case of poaching in this area, it's your team that responds and nothing is ever done. Your team rarely catches these guys. That's suspicious at best. Maybe you should give her one good reason why she should do anything more than request early leave and go?"

Tamala paled and shook her head, then laughed in a high unnatural pitch like she wasn't sure what to say, but she didn't disagree with Meghan's assessment. She glanced over her shoulder at Meghan, who waited for him to reply.

What more could he give them than the truth? He wanted Tamala to trust him. "I have nothing to do with this. I promise you that. My team does the best job they can. I understand your hesitation to trust my team. But I'm asking you to trust *me* to get you safely out of this situation." And he prayed she did because he'd never faced anything like this.

Soon Tamala would be outside his park. Hopefully, whoever this man was, he wouldn't follow her beyond the Yellowstone exit.

She gave a brief nod. "Fine. I'll write a report, but I'm leaving out any information that I may have seen him before because I can't identify him…yet. I have to think of my own safety, too."

Meghan threw up her hands in frustration, but Tamala held her ground.

He took a deep breath, satisfied. "That's a fair compromise. Will someone be there to protect you while you're outside the park?" He doubted the poacher would hunt her like a bear, but his behavior yesterday made Clint think it was a possibility.

"I'll figure out a way. I always do. Maybe, once I decide where to go, I could bring someone with me so I'm not alone. I haven't planned that far ahead yet." She shoved her hair behind her ear.

"Since the poacher didn't let the possibility of revealing his face deter him, I don't think having just anyone there would keep him away either. Want me to take you somewhere?" He'd prayed about letting himself form friendships with the people in Yellowstone, but offering to help with anything outside his job went well beyond his norm. Too much of his heart was stuck on complete honesty, not friendship, and the Lord had been nudging him to open up. He'd refused to listen until that moment.

"I think I'll manage. West Yellowstone has enough people that I won't be alone. No one can try anything, or I'll call the police. They'll be right there if I do. After that, I'll be far enough away that no one will follow. I can take a plane from the airport there."

He nodded and considered some friends on the West Yellowstone police department. "That's a good idea. You should file a report there, too." He laughed, hoping to lighten the tension coursing off Meghan.

Tamala pursed her lips instead of laughing and a realization hit him like a punch to the chest. His word wasn't enough. He'd have to prove to her he was trust-worthy. Angling his head toward the door, he silently asked her to follow him to his pickup, then headed to unlock the passenger door for her. He naturally glanced over the parking area, watching for anyone. Was she the missing piece to the whole poaching ring he'd been in-vestigating? She climbed into his pickup and he closed the door for her.

He reached for his walkie and turned it to the secure channel only he and Mark used. "Mark, we need a rush on the Hummer information." Once they knew who had rented the truck, he'd have a name.

Tamala had managed to escape easily when she'd been in the poacher's crosshairs and the truck had man-aged to disappear without a trace. Maybe she'd gotten away too easily.

THREE

Minutes seemed to take years, even though Clint checked her neck and pupils efficiently at the clinic. Tamala reluctantly walked with him toward his office. She wanted to catch the poacher, but everything within her warred with her decision to trust Clint temporarily.

He seated her across from him at his desk and she tugged the zipper on her coat down to get comfortable. "I can drive to West Yellowstone and fly out tomorrow if you can sign off on my early release."

With nowhere else to go, she prayed going home was safe. She'd need to pick up a few necessities before she left for Florida. "I'll go back and rest. Give your team time to catch this guy." She did her best to keep the doubt from her voice, but couldn't stop her glance from skipping to the open doorway. Mark sat just down the hall, clicking away at a computer, probably listening to their every word.

Everything she'd said to Clint had been the truth, but he seemed to think she knew more. If Meghan hadn't spoken up, he wouldn't even know of her own doubts. If her suspicions were true, and his team was in fact guilty, she'd only end up in a ditch faster.

He eyed her for a moment as he pulled the forms from his desk. "I'm hesitant about letting you just go on with your life as normal. Someone pointed a gun at you, ran us off the road, threatened you, and you simply want to drive away and take your chances? I think I'll feel much better when you're safely on a plane heading away from the park." He metered each word, like he'd practiced saying them ahead of time.

But was his concern real, or a smokescreen to cover up his involvement? If his uneasiness was genuine, why did he care? It wasn't like they were friends. She'd made sure she was always on her own. Even Meghan's support had seemed odd.

She'd wanted to keep the suspicions about his team to herself. That being said, the issue was out in the open now and he was the only person who could help her. He'd been close enough to see the build of the poacher, even if the accident had knocked him out. If they had a chance to ID a suspect after his apprehension, Clint might confirm or deny her choice, but only with her there to point at the right face.

"I want to go to Florida, but I *am* worried he'll follow me and put my parents in danger." Bringing this threat to Florida left her and her family wide open. She had to go into hiding somewhere no one would ever suspect. Where that might be was still a mystery, but Clint couldn't help her with that. If she decided to stay in Yellowstone and he knew about it, he could lose his job. There were many small towns in Wyoming, perfect for disappearing. A secluded cabin in Yellowstone Park, even though it was against the rules, would be easier. Either way, she'd have to choose fast.

"You're thinking about not going to your parents' home? Do you know someone in law enforcement you could report this to, to monitor you wherever you go? That alone might scare off any would-be attacker." His fingers thrummed a beat on his desk.

"I don't know anyone." Not to mention the hunter also saw Clint. *If* Clint wasn't working with the poacher, he was safer if she didn't mention anything in the report. Bravery might save him, even if it didn't save her, because without her presence, the threat against Clint was gone. He'd been on the ground and an easy target. So Clint wasn't who the poacher was after.

"Then I will take you to the airport. Simple decision. I'll get the sign-off in the next day or two. You should get out of the park anyway. The National Weather Service is talking about a storm coming in. It'll last for days. If you don't get out soon, you won't be able to get out at all for a while."

She nodded, filling in the report with what she remembered of the poacher, knowing that memories were vague and what she recalled could describe half the men she knew. She paused, thinking. The poacher wouldn't find her again if she didn't leave him a trail. In Yellowstone, there were perfect places she'd never be found. Meghan told her to hide, so she'd hide from her attacker *and* from Clint's team.

"I can't describe him beyond his build and face shape, nor remember the license plate. This is the report, but I feel like I'm wasting your time." She slid the papers toward him. There were other law enforcement rangers in other areas who would see it. "Now, can you keep your promise? If something happens to me, will you look into your own team?" She hated confrontation. It reminded her too much of the feelings that kept her in research and in the field, not on scientific panels where she had to talk, and especially away from relationships.

"I trust my team with my life." He glanced over the page and frowned. "I didn't realize you had a physical altercation with him."

She held the wave of nausea at bay. Just reliving that moment made the scene come back. "I kicked him twice and punched him. He stole my bear. I know that seems silly, but that bear was from my mom. She got it for me when she had cancer. She's well now, but that doesn't make it any less important."

He rested a hand over hers, sending warmth down her fingers. She should pull away. She didn't want to want his comfort, yet she couldn't bring herself to do it.

"I'm sorry. Can you describe it? If someone finds it, that could tell us where he's been."

She closed her eyes, picturing the tiny bear. "He was black with velvety fur, not fuzz. He had a little park ranger vest on with a matching hat." They had similar ones in the gift shop, but not the same. Not the one Mom had given her. "I know it's probably gone forever. But thank you for asking." She wiped her nose and shoved to her feet.

The window drew her and she stood, taking in the Tetons in the distance while she controlled her battered emotions.

"You can do this. But you don't have to do it alone." Clint's solid voice came from directly behind her.

Foolishly, she wanted to lean against him and let him be her strength for a little while. "I know I'm not alone. God will get me through this."

"He will. And I plan to be a vessel and help Him get the job done."

The window shattered in front of her, raining glass and prickling her face. Clint tackled her to the floor as another shot tore through the window, lodging in the opposite wall.

"Clint? Are you hurt?" His weight felt heavy on her, and she prayed now for his protection as well as hers.

Mark belly-crawled toward them down the hall and aimed at the window, his pistol ready should anyone try to enter.

Clint slowly raised himself off her, but didn't respond. He gripped her arm until she met his steely gaze. Without speaking, he nodded toward the door.

For a bare moment, she wasn't sure why he didn't just tell her what to do.

"Tamala, this way," Mark whispered. "We need to get you out of here."

Clint nodded his agreement and drew his gun, then slowly stood to the side of the window, out of range of whoever had been outside.

"I'm not going anywhere." She stalled. Clint had just saved her life. She'd been right next to that window and he'd been behind her. If that bullet hadn't missed, both of them could be dead. There was no way Clint could be one of the poachers. He never would've stood there, putting his own life in danger, if he were. "Clint, I trust you."

Clint scanned his office and wondered if he could get Tamala out without putting her within the line of sight of the window. At least he could see the trust in her eyes now. Though she still didn't trust Mark.

He couldn't fault her. He'd pored over every file of every naturalist, looking for some connection to the bear poaching. Whoever it was, he knew about the park. Intimately. Tamala might not be the connection, but the poacher was gunning for her. His gut shouted for him to protect her.

Though Tamala had given him her trust, she didn't trust his team, and that told him what he needed to know. There could be no friendship between them without complete trust. Not after losing his wife, Mary. He refused to entangle himself in anything *beyond* a friendship. Mary had loved him. They'd had a great life, and then she'd kept a secret that killed her. When she'd left for the winter season, she'd never returned. She hadn't told him about her aggressive cancer, or that she'd been told she only had a few weeks to live. If he'd only known, he could've at least prepared for her loss, but she hadn't even granted him the chance to hug her one last time, or say goodbye…

So much for love. He refused to let this brief spark with Tamala cloud his judgment any more than he already had. His heart wasn't ready to let anyone in.

He tucked her behind him, placing her hand at his waist and nodding for her to follow. Skirting around the room, he gave the barrel of his gun a slight twitch to the window so Mark knew he needed to take over at his place.

Just then, the all clear sounded outside. He wanted to relax, but poachers were stealthy. He couldn't let his guard down now. "We'll talk more when we get to the center of the building. My men will canvass the area while we talk," he whispered.

He took her to an enclosed conference room and then set his shoulder walkie on the table so he could be ready if any of his men needed him. "Are you now convinced that you need my help? Allow me to help you. Getting you to safety *is* my job." He hated arguing that her issue was work for him. The point-blank statement made his worry feel sterile. People who had been stalked or assaulted often felt guilt, and he didn't want her to.

"You can't." She shrugged, closing her eyes. "I'd be taking you away from the park. Mama needs your protection as much as I do."

He had to hold back the urge to reach for her hand. This wasn't about comfort. Why was he trying to comfort her? "I have men who are just as committed to the safety of each and every animal *and* human in our park. If this is where I'm needed most, it's what I'll do." Maybe now his words would instill more trust between them.

She didn't speak immediately, and trying to gauge her thoughts proved difficult. He couldn't see her emotions as she kept her head bent, studying her fingers folded in front of her. The silence spread between them.

"You've already gotten in too deep by helping me. The park service would never agree to this. I don't want to see anyone point a gun at you again." She finally met his eyes and her jaw firmed.

Tamala had a backbone. He'd give her that. "Well, I didn't appreciate him aiming a gun at you either. At least I'm trained to defend against him." His need to protect those around him ran deep, and failing to defend her twice now weighed heavy on his shoulders.

There wasn't time for waiting. "You had a gun aimed at you. If my officer hadn't shown up the exact moment he did, I'd be digging through your file to find your family. Let me deal with the park service." Offering to talk to the park service would also bolster the trust between him and Tamala. She might not trust his team like he did, but there was no question where the park service's allegiance was.

She took a deep breath and let it out, her shoulders relaxing just slightly as if she were physically giving him some of the weight lying on her. "Okay. You're right. If I'm going to trust you, I need to show it, not just say it. What do we do from here?"

He resisted the urge to smile, but her acceptance felt like a victory. "I'm going to call and put in your request to leave due to an emergency. I'm going to tell them I need to deliver you to the airport in West Yellowstone. That's not a question. When I'm done with the call, I'm going to escort you back to your barracks, where you can pack."

There was a sharp knock on the door and Clint responded quickly, "Enter."

Mark strode in with a clear plastic baggie, a shell casing inside, and set it on the table. "Looks like he was lying on the ground about forty yards from your window. He must have pulled up and left the moment he shot. All we found was the casing and the trampled spot where he'd been lying. And this." He laid a candy bar wrapper on the table. "Might get a print off of it."

Tamala stared at the table and furrowed her brow.

"What is it?"

She shook her head as if what she thought was silly. "Nothing. I hope you get some prints off it and we can all return to business as normal."

He picked up the shell casing. It was from a high-powered rifle. Professional, like snipers used. And looked to be the same as the one they'd found at the scene with Tamala's attempted murder. If they didn't catch this guy fast, life might never be normal for her again.

FOUR

The next day, back in her dark living room, Tamala waited behind a locked door for Clint to arrive to take her to the airport. She researched on her computer for any information on Mama Bear 228, and anyone seen hunting her. The faint glow of the screen acted as the only light. Since the attack, she'd been afraid to let anyone know when she was home. That meant leaving the lights off and paying attention to her surroundings. She'd been told to call for Clint or Mark anytime she'd needed to leave, not that she had. Her home felt like the one and only safe place in Yellowstone.

A loud bang split the silence outside her door. She jumped and slapped her computer closed, reaching for her phone. Hopefully, her computer had saved what she'd found. On a normal day, before the attack, she wouldn't have been alone in employee housing at that hour. She'd have been out in the park. There was no reason for anyone to be out there.

She pressed the button on her cell phone screen to turn off her hot spot and sent a text to Clint, then crept to the door. The lock was engaged. Her heart hoped

Clint had made the noise, but she'd be a fool to trust that hope. A prayer escaped her lips in a soft murmur of protection. *Lord, I know I'm not supposed to fear, but I'm frightened...*

The knob jiggled and turned, then broke with one crunching blow. She grabbed her computer off the table as she scanned the room for a place to hide. For once, she was thankful for her petite frame as she settled on the only spot available, an end table.

The mid-sized table was vintage 80s, picked up from a thrift store. Its entire center was hollow for storage. Climbing inside, she curled up into a tight ball, the space so close she struggled to tug the door shut in front of her.

Most of the time, she forgot about the table, and she hoped whoever came in would, too. The cabinet was octagonal and the closure became almost invisible once shut. Since she didn't have a back door and no time to climb out a window, hiding was her only option.

She clutched her computer to her chest from her cramped position and scrunched her eyes closed, listening as a few men stomped inside. Gruff voices mumbled above her head. Footsteps clomped around her. Closer, then farther away. Her stomach roiled, and she bit her lip to keep from screaming whenever they drew near.

"Looks like she's not here. Her truck is outside, so I was sure she'd be inside. Search the place. Under the bed, in the fridge. Anywhere she might fit," the rough voice wasn't familiar. How many men could be working with the poacher, or was this some other attack?

Tamala prayed her trembling wouldn't make the end table visible and they wouldn't hear her heavy breathing. They stomped back to her bedroom, obviously not worried about noise. The invasion into her private home hit her like a punch. She allowed no one in her bedroom. And here they were, violating her space in so many ways.

Cabinet doors slammed nearby, then came the crash of breaking dishes. Her filing cabinet hit the floor with a metal-mangling crunch right next to her hiding place, shaking the floor beneath her. Smacking her mouth tight and swallowing her fear as best she could, she clutched close to her computer. If they found her, and especially if they saw what she'd been searching for, they wouldn't be any less rough. One of them had pulled a gun on her already.

If they toppled the table and she fell out, they'd kill her before she could escape. There had to be more to this invasion than seeing one of their faces. This felt personal.

Above all the destruction, the men laughed and made more threats. "She must be out for a walk with Clint. There's no way she's hiding anywhere in here. We'll wait outside until she gets back. If she's done any nosing around, she might find enough to know who I am. I can't let her tell anyone. You guys get out of here. I belong here, you don't. I can find out what she knows."

Tamala sucked in a gasp. He'd called Clint by name. He said he belonged here… She bit her lip and prayed for help. There was a whole team of men after her, and she hadn't come up with anyone in her search who matched her memory. Nor could she figure out why he'd looked familiar. She wasn't as acquainted with the rangers in other areas of the park, but Clint would be.

One of the other men growled to her right. "If we let her get away, the hunting endorsements will stop. All those hunting trips to Africa we planned and the ad campaigns for the rifles, *poof.* We'd better hide the truck. She'll remember it when she comes back. If she sees that, she'll run."

"Twenty-five million reasons to make sure we never get caught." He laughed. "We'll pin the poaching on Clint and his team, proving the rumors true, and the poaching will stop since we'll move on. We get all the fame and money, never go to jail and we can continue to hunt. Without her, there's nothing in our way."

That was him. The man who'd pulled a gun on her. But who were the others? He'd been alone the day she'd encountered him. None of them sounded familiar, like the rangers she worked with in the Old Faithful area.

"That's my job, my brother."

Tamala held her breath as sweat dripped down her neck. The man who'd threatened her might be anyone. Her mind swirled. Where could she go? Because if she survived, she couldn't stay in this hiding spot forever.

"Todd and Danny, go hide the truck."

She waited, listening for any other useful information. Meghan, in all her seemingly overdramatic worry, and Clint, in his protective way, had been right. She needed to leave Yellowstone as soon as possible.

"Maybe she has a hiding place for her computer? Somewhere she stores it all day? We should check the usual places, between folded towels, under the mattress… Without that, she can't find or report anything. Would you look at all this bear stuff? She might know where the bears are better than we do." Her attacker's voice came closer as her cabin door slammed again. Probably the men he'd called Todd and Danny leaving.

The compliment left her cold. How long had they been in her park? How had they known right where to find her? She hadn't had her own truck until she'd returned Clint to his house, so they couldn't have looked for that to find her. That was even more proof that these men had access to everything in the park, including her records. They knew what was in the report she'd written. Shivers wracked her body.

After what seemed like forever, the sounds stopped. Her ears strained to hear where the men were, but she refused to move until she could be certain they were gone. Her body ached in the cramped position, and she silently counted to keep calm, but no noise penetrated the table. Was the quiet a trap? The silence was almost worse than the noise of the destruction. She'd sent a text to Clint. Where was he?

Throbbing in her knees and back meant she'd sat cramped for a long time, but if she moved too soon, she might be dead. If she *didn't* move soon, she wouldn't be able to get out of the table without help. These men knew Clint… But what if the knowledge was one-sided? Or did she just want to believe she could find some safety in this hysteria? Being with Clint had felt safe, secure. Even when she hadn't trusted him.

The poacher spoke first, and she bit her fist to hold in any noise. "Nothing. She must have her computer with her. We'll break into her truck if we can and check there, then I'll wait outside," came the voice she recognized.

"You can't sit here long. This is a no visitor area. While we can follow her pretty much anywhere else in the park, this is one place we're definitely not supposed to be. Keep your eyes peeled. I don't want to get kicked out of the park and have to find another way in for you."

As soon as her door slammed shut the second time, Tamala kicked open the door to her hiding spot and unfolded from the small table. An eternity had passed waiting for those men to leave, and she was so stiff her body hurt to move. Her breathing came ragged as she hunched on her knees, taking in all they'd done.

Destruction surrounded her. Tables lay in pieces. Other smashed furniture littered the floor. Her filing cabinet, with all her bear studies and research, lay on its side. The contents spilled out and spread everywhere. Her hiding place had been one of the few things they didn't destroy, and she thanked God again for His protection. They'd missed her completely.

Though the window cover was only a light roman shade, she knew the men were out there. Unless she went near the window, she would remain unseen. Picking her way through the rubble, she rushed to her front door and tried to lock it, but the knob hung limp and broken.

The slam of a car door caught her attention, and she maneuvered herself next to the window to see outside. The men had left and the only truck besides her own in the lot was Clint's silver pickup. Fatigue and worry washed over her. He would pack her up and send her right out of the park if he saw her room, and she still had nowhere to go besides her parents' home.

If she let him inside, he'd see the destruction and chaos. There was no hiding the mess.

He knocked. "Tam, are you in there?" The broken knob jiggled. "Tamala? I'm coming in!"

Clint pulled his gun and kept it pointed down.

Her yellow truck sat alone in the lot, bright and obvious. No other cars or people around gave any indication of what had happened here. Nothing had been reported.

He had her papers with him, approving her early departure from the park. If she was packed, they would leave.

Tamala yanked open her door enough for him to see her face, but not inside her cabin. She didn't look him in the eye and her pretty face appeared mottled and shiny like she'd been sweating heavily.

"I'm glad you're here. They came." She glanced all around the parking area, avoiding his gaze.

He holstered his gun to keep from frightening her further. "They?"

She nodded. "At least three of them. I lost track of all their voices."

Clint radioed Mark and filled him in then turned his attention back to Tamala. "I just saw your message— it didn't come through right away. I was worried." As much as he didn't want to sound like an officer, or that he cared overmuch, he was and did. Her safety was his job and despite hunting all over his jurisdiction all morning, no one had seen a black Hummer. This guy seemed one step ahead of him at every turn.

She bit her lip and pulled the door tighter to her body. "I'm ready to go when you are."

While that was great news, he saw a woman hiding something huge. Why wouldn't she look him in the eye? "You know, I think that accident may have hurt you more than you think. Maybe I should take you to a doctor in West Yellowstone before the airport. We should go to the clinic there, have them do an extensive check because something is amiss with your vision." He pointed to the broken handle and waited to see her reaction.

Pain filled her face before she ducked her head. "I don't need to go anywhere besides the airport." She shook her head wildly for a moment, then gripped the door and closed her eyes.

"I need to get you out of here. Now. Grab your bags and then we can discuss exactly what you should do after you reach Florida. There's a big storm moving in and I want you in the air before they stop flights. One of those named blizzards. I want to make sure you're out before we have to do the rigmarole of clearing everyone from the park who won't want to leave and getting vehicles off the roads before this storm." If he laid out everything they would do, then she would know he trusted her. "Listen, I know you're scared. I would be, too." A little truth he wouldn't normally share might break the ice. "Please, let me in."

She pressed her eyes with the heels of her palms, letting the door swing slightly. "Let me grab my bags. Just wait here."

Her trembling tugged at something deep inside him. Something he hadn't felt in a long time. "Not a question. You just said they were nearby. I'm not leaving you alone." She still didn't trust him enough for that tiny request? He'd thought they were past that.

"I'll grab my purse and bag. It's just right here." She backed away and closed the door in his face.

Was she hiding something having to do with the poachers or was she suddenly shy? He backed away from the door and tried not to get frustrated. She'd said she trusted him. She'd called for help. What had happened that she now obviously felt the need to guard herself?

He only had two days at most to discover who the poacher—and now his accomplices—were before the biggest storm since he'd become a ranger beat down on them and trapped whoever remained in the park.

Where had the men gone? She glanced over her shoulder, looking in Clint's rearview mirror, waiting for the Hummer to follow them. Adrenaline had to explain what made her shake like a paint mixer. She might pass off her trembling as hunger, but her stomach rejected the idea of eating. Bottom line, she was not in law enforcement and had no training to handle an aggressive situation with criminals like she had, nor how to handle the aftermath. Maybe Clint was right and she did need a doctor. But first, she needed to tell him the poacher knew who he was.

The longer she sat in the cab of Clint's pickup, the more certain she was that her time on earth would draw to a quick close if she didn't find help somewhere.

Her parents weren't prepared to take on poachers and killers any more than she was. They didn't understand her normal job at Yellowstone, and she didn't even fully understand how a poacher could turn deadly. The police might help, but poaching was usually covered by the fish and wildlife branch, so they might not understand in the same way Clint would.

Clint was known by the poacher, but not connected with him. Keeping him by her side put his life on the line, but did she have any choice? She'd pushed him back, but by being with her, he'd find himself a target either way. If Clint had been a part of the poaching ring, he wouldn't have come to her door right after the poachers had been there and the poachers wouldn't have shot out his window. He'd want her alone, not to help her.

"I know I've been saying I can do this on my own, but…" She closed her eyes and prayed for the right words.

"But you don't want to," he finished for her.

He'd given her a lifeline. A way to ask for help without being needy. "Correct. I didn't let you into my home back there because they came and ransacked it. I was scared. Embarrassed. Unsure how I felt or what to do. And," she paused and took a deep breath, "I hid while they destroyed everything."

He yanked off the road so quickly she had to brace herself against the dashboard. "You were there? Are you hurt?" He threw the truck in Park, pressed the emergency flashers and waited, looking her over at the same time.

She clutched her hands to stop the shaking, but the more she acknowledged that she'd be dead if they'd found her, the harder they shook. "I hid in a table. They didn't damage that. Everything else…" She fought control as tears spilled down her cheeks over the utter mess and loss of all they'd broken.

"Tam, we need to get you on that plane. Where else could you go?"

She wished her answer held more choices than one. "I have nowhere."

FIVE

Car lights zoomed by, the first she'd noticed all night, and she gripped the armrest, waiting for the car to pass them. After either going to the clinic or the airport, she'd have to deal with being alone. They'd found her home. At some point, when she could return, she'd have to clean up her entire cabin. She yawned and fought drowsiness.

"I don't know what to do. Right now, I can't keep my thoughts straight. I don't know where to go or who to trust." She massaged her aching temples.

Clint took a deep breath and stared ahead. "I misread your actions earlier as a concussion when I now realize you're dealing with an adrenaline and stress overload. I'm sorry about that." He glanced at his watch. "We may need to find somewhere safe for you to stay tonight if we don't hurry." He turned to glance in the rearview mirror, then back to her. "Tell me what you know, because you may have heard something we can use to figure out who they are."

Tamala heard the words he didn't say. He wanted her to trust him, really trust him. Her suspicion that Clint's team was in on the poaching ring needn't be said. She was certain he wasn't, and mentioning the past would only cause anger. She needed him on her side, not resenting her.

"I told you they were in my bungalow. But I didn't tell you that whoever the head poacher is, he knew you by name. He said if I poked around too much, I'd find him online…" Even as she said it, she wracked her brain for any similarities she might have overlooked to people she knew. Yellowstone held fundraisers to help the wildlife. Would the poachers come to one of those just to find out more information?

"You think he wants to silence you because there's more than an arrest on the line, and someone like me recognizing him is dangerous to his end goal?" Clint leaned against the truck window in thought. "Interesting. Didn't see that coming."

"Yes, much more than just an arrest. He said something about millions of dollars and endorsements. He has been the poacher all along, but if the poachers frame your team and you're all arrested and the poaching stops, they get a massive reward from a private conservation group." She couldn't believe that, in a bid to save the bears, the group would end up hurting them.

"The bears are one of the main reasons I chose Yellowstone," she said. The fact was, with her degree and extensive knowledge, she far exceeded the requirements for the naturalist job. She had the qualifications to work in any park, but Yellowstone had been her dream. "So if this person actually attends any of Yellowstone's many fundraisers and the pictures of attendees are online, I might eventually recognize him if I hunt for his face.

I don't know if it helps, because I don't recognize the names, but two of the men with him, he called Todd and Danny."

He took a moment to think. "I'll check my records for anyone with those names who might be connected. So, how can we use this information? He won't do anything where people or our wildlife cameras can see him and catch his face." Despite yanking them off the road, his calm now relaxed her.

Though she'd fought telling him, there was no one to hear a thing out in the middle of nowhere in his truck. She felt safer there than she had in the last two days.

"Most years, while you stay during the winter season here, I go to Florida and study the information I collect the rest of the year on Yellowstone bear habits and poaching. I've never come face-to-face with an actual poacher, but I have to believe this is different. After all my studies, no one has targeted me before."

His brow furrowed, and he took a moment before he answered. "That still doesn't answer the question. We know he's someone whose face would be known to me and not you. And he's worried you'll figure out who he is. That's why he's trying to silence both of us. I might know his name if I saw him, but you could confirm he's the poacher."

Outwitting killers wasn't in her usual job description. Her actual research hadn't led her to the poacher. Mama Bear 228 and her love of that bear had. "I feel like if he's that worried I'll ID him, he'll follow me out of the park."

"Agreed, but if he doesn't follow us out of the park, then it's likely he won't find us. He might know me, but he doesn't know you or where you'll go. I don't want you trapped here."

"But what about you? If I leave, will he turn his focus on you?"

"He's threatened you. Once you're safely in hiding, I can work with my team better. I can focus our efforts." Clint glanced outside as random flakes began to fall. "We're getting close to the point of no return with this weather. Let's get you to West Yellowstone, near the airport. You can stay the night. I'll have the police watch your hotel and escort you to the airport in the morning."

"Have you thought about letting me stay? I know the park service doesn't allow it, but I have no other options where I'm not alone. I would be around you, who knows the danger. If he knows the rules, he'd expect I would follow them and leave."

The park service wasn't one to grant special requests, but the season wasn't technically over yet. If she rode out the storm in Yellowstone, she might be able to leave safely once the park service cleared the roads for travel. The poacher would have nowhere to ride out the storm. He might remain in the park, but the wise plan would be to leave. Biding her time *might* actually be the safest course.

"I don't know. Not without approval and I'd never get that in time. Where could you stay that still had heat?"

She bit her lip, considering her options. Yellowstone used mostly electric heat, which was turned off when it wasn't needed. The only exceptions were the warming houses, some of which had wood stoves. At least he hadn't just said no to her staying.

Clint continued, "With the threat of this blizzard

looming, we've been telling day visitors they might not be able to get back in. The National Park Service will shut down roads for this one, so I'm waiting for word to close the park completely. The concessioners are sending their nonessential workers home early. I don't want people stranded. I'm hearing this will be a major snowfall. Possibly the worst I've ever seen."

Yellowstone usually closed for only a day or two because of bad weather, then opened again until the last day of the season. Sending people home early made her wonder if they'd bother calling anyone back. "Will they open for snow vehicles?" The park closed from various dates in late October until mid-March for anything except vehicles made for snow once the snowpack was deep enough.

He shrugged slightly, though the movement was difficult to see in the dark truck and with his heavy coat. "I assume so, but I'll get my direction from the NPS. I don't make the rules. Most of these early snows are no more than a dusting, followed by severe cold. We've had some cold, which usually keeps the snow away. This heat is causing the volatility. Pray for cold."

She'd heard him mention prayer before and his comment, though offhand, reassured her. "What about the poachers?"

She still didn't want to really think of them, but since they were talking about the park, she had to know. "Do you think they'll try to stay behind in the snow? Is right now the best time for me to escape?" If she stayed in West Yellowstone, or in Mammoth Hot Springs, where the lodging remained open later than in other places in the park, she might escape the poachers, since they wouldn't know where she was. They didn't even know her name. Then, Clint could come pick her up again after the snow closure and the threat was gone. But that would leave her alone, with no help if the poachers found her.

"We'll scan the entire park as much as possible. People who don't leave are in grave danger. If the snow doesn't melt right away, we won't be able to get to some areas for a while. We check every vehicle when it comes into Yellowstone against illegal camping, etcetera, so they can't bring in enough equipment to survive this. There's nowhere to hide them. Only the remote rangers have the room to store what they'd need to survive for at least a week. They've already planned to be in place for months."

She shivered. While staying in an isolated location sounded like bliss to some people, literally seeing no one for a few months at a time would tax even her abilities. "Too much alone time. Even as a naturalist who loves quiet, I wouldn't love that."

"The hotel near the airport will work for now. I'll get some help and make sure they board up your house and secure it," he stated.

"I wish I'd managed to keep silent when I saw him. If he hadn't seen me…" Then she wouldn't be relying on Clint right now.

"*If* doesn't do anyone any good. You got yourself out of the situation without injury. Now we'll deal with the aftermath." He gave her a reassuring glance.

With Clint's help, she'd find a safe place to hide that the poacher and his men didn't know about. She might finally have a moment to think.

* * *

Clint drove, trying to concentrate on the road while considering all the things Tamala said and trying to ignore his own feelings. She'd finally trusted him. Only him. Her parents didn't know where she was or what she was facing. Though he still didn't know the name of the main poacher, he now had something. Tamala didn't know any more either, but if they both worked together, he had no doubt they'd figure out who the poacher was.

He refused to think how worried he was at leaving her in a hotel forty miles away from where he could watch over her. She was scared, shaking and nervous about what she'd said. Finding somewhere safe was the only thing to consider. The situation was forcing him to really consider her question of allowing her to stay with him despite the rules.

Clint wasn't sure how the poachers had tracked down Tamala's cabin, but the park planners didn't set Yellowstone up for security from an attack like this. He had to think like a poacher to figure out where they were hiding out and how they had tracked Tamala down. The only things in the park people tried to avoid were dangerous animal encounters, and even those not that well. Yellowstone didn't invest in a lot of lights or security other than his team and the rangers in the other Yellowstone areas. Neither the rangers, nor their teams, oversaw every area of the park all at once. It was a delicate balance—keeping park visitors and staff safe while maintaining the natural splendor of Yellowstone.

"How much damage did they do?" He hated to think about her sitting there in hiding as men tore her home apart around her. She had to have been terrified.

He caught her shiver out of the corner of his eye as she nodded. "There's a lot of damage."

No wonder she was shaken up. She'd sat there silently while they ripped apart everything she loved. "I'll help you clean up." He'd barely spoken the words before he heard a *pop* and glass rained down over them as his rear window exploded in.

"They're shooting at us!" she said as she covered her head. He tugged her down out of view as he scanned the area. He couldn't see lights behind them and realized whoever it was must have similar training as he did. Driving at night without lights was a skill he'd learned in law enforcement training.

"Clint?" Tam looked up at him with wide eyes. He wanted to reassure her, but more than that, he wanted to get her somewhere he could be sure to protect her and that *wasn't* two hours away on the minimum speed roads. The hotel wasn't going to work. It was time to consider plan B.

He cranked the wheel, heading back in the direction they'd come, and his headlights caught the reflection of the truck as it zoomed by. He revved the engine, racing for the next secluded area where he could hide until he was sure they were gone.

A band of trees lay just ahead and he pulled in, then rolled down his window as he drew his pistol, waiting for the Hummer to follow them. After ten of the longest minutes of his life, he drew a deep breath. "I think they're gone."

She shook her head. "I'm not staying alone in West Yellowstone."

He had to agree. "No, for tonight, you're staying with me."

After a frigid drive and a quick scan of the area near Tamala's house, he pulled in. He saw no sign of the big black truck. The dim overhead lights showed a few vehicles parked in the lot, but all were people he knew to work in the park and had a visible park sticker. Unless the poacher had people working in Clint's department, they were safe for a while. "We'll go in, secure your door and get out. Nothing more."

Meghan's car was missing, and he recalled how vehement she'd been about Tamala leaving. "Did your neighbor leave already?" That late in the evening, she should've finished for the day.

"Meghan should be here." Tamala searched the area. "I should've left her a note. She probably saw the knob, went in and saw the mess, then headed for your office to report it."

He parked his truck then led her to the front door. Pressing the call button on his shoulder walkie, he radioed into the office. "Anyone report vandalism in the naturalist housing area?"

The radio crackled and whined. Finally, dispatch answered, "None today."

He paused to think. Meghan might not have followed her usual routine, but if she had, the state of Tamala's house should've alarmed her. Unless the poachers had gotten to her, thinking they had Tamala. Both were dark haired and about the same height. That's where the similarity ended, but virtual strangers wouldn't know that.

As he stepped inside, the destruction left him speechless. They would need hours to clean up what the men had to have done in minutes. "Let's hurry. I'll get the door, grab anything you may have forgotten."

She nodded and rushed back to her room.

He stared at the mangled kitchen table. The guys had been angry, judging by the damage. "I'm so thankful they didn't find you," Clint said as Tamala returned, shoving the last item in a backpack and slinging it over her shoulder. The longer she was there, the more visibly shaken she became.

As he watched her, he regretted bringing her here. Her apprehension made him nervous and watching outside split his focus from helping her. But if they hadn't come, he wouldn't have realized Meghan was gone. He hated to make her aware of the possibility, but Meghan had to be reported missing.

"I don't want to leave all of this for them…" She clutched her stomach, then picked up a broken bear mug off the floor. "My father bought this…" she mumbled.

"Time to leave." He gently took the mug from her and set it on the counter. Anyone might be watching them through the windows with the lights on and his neck tingled with the feeling of eyes on him. Their window of possible safety was quickly closing.

"Let's get out of here right now. Leave this for me. I'll clean up as I can while the park is empty." He pressed the call button on his walkie. "Command? Be on the lookout for Meghan Dale. Unless she's reported in, she appears to be missing."

"Ten four, Dale has not been in contact. I'll send Mark over to her residence now."

Tamala leaned on him, so sleepy she struggled to keep her eyes open. The attack had worn her out completely. He fought the urge to lay a hand on her back to guide her, then gave in to the temptation. She settled in at his side and he pulled his gun as they reached the door. "Stay next to me and if you hear or see anything, run for the truck and drive."

He took her bag from her then ushered her out to the truck and opened the door. The cab of the truck was too cold with the missing window and the falling temperatures. She climbed into hers and settled, tucking her hands between her knees. "We'll go to your house. Then what?"

"Then we'll hunker down and plan." If only it were that easy.

SIX

Only a short ride to Clint's house. Tamala blinked rapidly to stay awake and focus on any movement around her. No one else was out and the park was mostly shrouded in darkness. Tiny flakes of snow reflected in the overhead lights. She was really being hunted and nothing about it felt real.

Had it really been less than an hour since someone had shot at them?

A *pop* broke the silence and Clint's truck lost all control, careening off the road and down into a shallow ditch. Clint gripped the wheel, trying to remain in control. Her mind froze and she reached for the door to escape, but questioned if that was the smartest thing to do. Someone had just shot out their tire. She wasn't going to be any safer outside of the truck.

Clint gripped her shoulder and pushed her down, covering her with his body. She couldn't see or hear anything, but the pounding of her heartbeat in her ears.

"I'm getting out to look around. Do not move." He pulled his gun as he slowly backed away from her.

She huddled on the floorboard, praying that the whole situation would end soon. Clint hadn't even closed the door before he fired three shots in rapid succession. Another bullet lodged in his truck, a black hole in the extended cab behind Clint's seat the only remaining evidence. She yelled, covering her head. "Clint!" He was out there alone and the only protection he had was his gun.

Tamala forced herself to peer over the seat to find Clint. With careful aim, he took two more shots. She didn't know much about handguns, but he couldn't have many bullets left and there might be more than one man.

He dodged off the road and into the trees. She'd been with him long enough to know he would normally call in for help, but he couldn't call in now or risk talking and giving away his location. She had to act as his partner. She found his walkie where it had fallen on the floor when they'd skidded off the road and pressed the button.

"Yellowstone Law Enforcement Ranger Station, over," came an all-business voice.

The sound seemed overly loud to her ears. "Yes, this is Tamala Roth. I'm on the side of the road near Grand Loop. Clint is with me. Someone is shooting at us." If only she knew who that someone was.

She heard something that sounded like clicking in the background. "We'll have a car on the way there shortly."

Clint came back suddenly and slid in the driver's side. He eyed his walkie and she handed it to him. After a short conversation describing what they'd been through, he clipped it back on his shoulder.

"My truck tire is blown. They ran back into the trees and I couldn't find tracks in the dark and didn't want to leave you too long. Keep your head down. I can limp the truck to my place, but it'll be slow. We'll figure out what to do from there. Pray we make it."

From the moment she'd met him three years ago, she'd thought he was amazingly handsome. His light brown hair and friendly dark blue eyes helped, but what made him irresistible was his love and respect for the things that mattered. Now more than ever. But never had she allowed herself to get to know him.

He'd mentioned prayer a few times now, which meant he was a believer. If she weren't on the run for her life, he would be the kind of guy she might choose. Maybe *the* one. Assuming he wasn't like every other guy she'd met and turn terrified once she used her brain full strength.

After a few bumpy minutes, he helped her out of the truck and carefully led her to his home, gun still at the ready and fully alert. Once inside, he bolted the door and she felt the weight of running fall from her shoulders, even if it was only temporary.

"Help yourself to anything in the kitchen," he said as he clicked the magazine release on his pistol, letting it fall into his hand.

Careful not to turn on lights so the house would look empty, she went to the kitchen and opened the fridge so she could find her way around his unfamiliar kitchen. Cheese and crackers would make a good, quick snack. Then she'd go to bed and try to rest for tomorrow.

The cupboard yielded a few slices of bread and a toaster. Close enough. She slathered the toast in butter, finished her snack quickly, and waited for Clint to tell her where to go.

He showed her where everything was in his split-level home which was small, but still more spacious than her cabin and neat as a pin.

"I'd like you to stay in my room for tonight. I'll take the couch where I can guard the front door." He stepped back, scraping his hand across the back of his neck. "I'm sorry we couldn't get you out of here."

They'd been ambushed twice and Clint had kept her alive. She couldn't exactly complain. "I'm here and breathing, right?" she said as she followed him to the door of his room.

He nodded his good-night and she closed the door, then took a deep breath as she flipped the light on. The uniform hanging on the door behind her gave off Clint's scent, and she closed her eyes, allowing herself to imagine what it would be like to have a guy like him around all the time, not just in an emergency.

Along two walls of the room ran a built-in shelf about three feet off the ground. She remembered going down a few steps to get in and realized they were basically in a basement. Along the shelf were pictures and awards Clint had received over the years. Her curiosity was too much, and she was too anxious after being shot at, yet again, to lie down. She might never again get the chance to find out about him.

There were awards for conservation and management, letters from important people that he'd received then framed, a picture with the new law enforcement ranger of the Mammoth Hot Springs area, and a picture of him with a woman in front of a bison calf. She picked the image up to get a closer look. Clint was a little younger, but not much, and the woman had her arm draped around him with a toothy smile. They looked happy and comfortable together.

Tamala knew Clint was single right now, but jealousy clenched at her insides and wouldn't let go. She forced her eyes closed. He had a right to have a past, and she had *no* right to his heart at the moment. Not even now, after his help. A permanent relationship wouldn't ever be part of her life since men never liked her type.

Wind and chill swirled in the room as the poacher's now familiar voice crept up her spine. "I'd hoped to get out of this park before the storm, but you won't play nice."

His hand clasped over her mouth before she could make a sound. He turned her around to face the way he'd come, stealing her chance to get a good look at his face. The screen lay on the ground outside and the window stood open just enough for him to slip through. She hadn't thought to lock the window. If he left with her, Clint wouldn't know until it was too late. How could he know where they were going?

He chuckled softly and whispered, "Scream and Clint dies along with you." His muffled speech held no discernible accent. He had to be local.

If she knew his exact stance, she might be able to get the upper hand and fight her way free. As he moved her, she kept her eyes down, trying to figure out where he placed his feet, how tall he was and what she could use to get away. He wore expensive cowboy boots, the kind that cost a fortune, with one deep colored blotch near the toe that set her trembling.

He bent in, too close. His nose mere inches from her neck and he rested a hand possessively on her, pinning her. His voice was a low, rumbling rasp. "You will not get away this time."

His hand clenched tighter over her mouth then slid down to her neck, choking her. She struggled to breathe, and her body forced a cough to free her airway, but that only made him tighten his grip.

As her heart slammed erratically, her mind raced. How could she get away, alert Clint, anything that would bring an end other than the one the killer wanted.

He slithered a single finger down her arm, toward the gun she knew had to be at his belt and she trembled. "I warned you I wasn't finished with you. You know too much."

When he drew a knife from his belt, not the gun she'd expected, her breath came in short rasps.

He held it up where she could see the long blade. "Let's get down to business."

A soft squeak of a cough startled Clint from his watch where he waited on the chair in his living room. Was the noise the floor, a mouse or a person? His brain fired before his body and he stood stiffly, taking in the vicinity in a heartbeat. His focus zeroed in on the swath of light under his bedroom door. Tamala was awake and obviously too tired to remember not to turn on the light.

Her exhaustion had been obvious before she'd gone to his room, and she was smart enough to know they had a long day ahead of them. Not to mention, a light on was like a beacon in the sleepy park. The poachers knew what truck he drove now, finding her wouldn't be difficult. He shook off his exhaustion.

Edging his way across the room, he grabbed his gun

at his side. A freezing cold draft swept over his feet. He took care to never open his window in his room. Living on ground level, any animal could try to push its way in. There were plenty of things in the park that didn't belong in his bedroom. On quick silent feet, he made his way down the hall, back to the wall and gun at the ready. The slightest hint of a man's voice gripped his attention, raspy, quiet, threatening.

Needles of apprehension ignited his shoulders, and he pressed his ear to the door.

"I could have made this quick for your sake, but you kept me here long past the time I wanted to be." The voice was familiar. Too familiar. But from where?

Tamala whimpered softly but didn't cry out. "I don't know who you are. I won't look. I'll just leave. Let me go." She squealed like the beginning of a smothered scream.

"Let you go? Where you'll soon forget how frightened you are at this moment? Where you can take everything I've ever worked for?"

Clint didn't need to hear more, but how to stop the situation and not make it worse? There was no way to know what kind of weapon the man had, but he had to have something or Tamala would likely fight back.

His training kicked in. There was a standard procedure for this kind of thing and just putting himself into the situation might save her life. He slowly opened the door, but they were behind it, in the area he couldn't see. Someone yanked the knob from his hands.

"Clint, run! It's the poacher, and he's got a knife," Tamala shrieked. She used the distraction to free herself and ran for the open window. At least he'd managed that.

The man grabbed his arm and wrenched him around, landing a punch to the side of his face. His vision went fuzzy for a moment, and Clint tried to anticipate where to block another blow. In a blurry whirl, something hard slammed into the side of his head, sending him to his knees. Where was Tamala? Had she made it to safety?

He fought against the growing darkness closing in as the poacher raced for the window. He had to see the guy's face. If he knew Clint, maybe the opposite would also be true. He blinked to clear his vision as he reached for his gun, but his movements felt slow as time stopped. "Freeze." He knew he sounded weak, but he needed to give Tamala time to run.

The poacher stalled for a moment as he climbed to the window, the darkness outside helped to shadow his face.

"I'll shoot if you don't stop." He might miss today, but Clint wouldn't give up until this man was behind bars.

The man started to slip through the open window and Clint aimed, but his vision doubled. He concentrated, but his training warned him not to shoot when he couldn't see his target.

The next thing he knew Tamala stood next to him, shaking him gently. "Clint, I got away from him. You gave me enough time. I waited until I saw him run toward my bungalow then came back. Are you all right?"

Was he? His head rang like a clanging bell.

"You okay to drive?" he asked, certain he wasn't, though he wasn't sure where they would go now. A dark, blurry line around his vision would make driving impossible, but at least he'd done his job of keeping Tam alive—for now.

She helped him up off the floor and grabbed the bag she'd packed from the kitchen before they headed outside. They scrambled into coats and out to his truck. With no back window and a flat tire they were stranded. Tamala shuffled them to her nearby truck, throwing off the tarp someone had used to hide it. She tossed it in Reverse and drove away quickly. Her eyes shifted every which way and her mouth hung open slightly. "I don't know where to go and the snow is coming down so hard I can't see." She shivered.

He could do little more than nod as he tried to concentrate on a course of action.

"Thank you for coming for me. I don't know what I would've done if you hadn't." She swallowed so hard he heard the noise in the close cab. "He said he'd kill me." The words squeaked from her throat.

He wished he could take some of her worry away. Instead, he could try to keep her safe. He glanced in the rearview to see if anyone followed them. So far, there were no lights or vehicles nearby. She pulled to the side of the road. "Clint, I can't keep driving without knowing where to go."

Something about the scene didn't sit well. He went over what happened in his head. "How did he find you? He'd followed you to your housing, but no one followed us to mine."

She closed her eyes tight. "He followed your pickup. He told me that's how he knew where I was. He knew which room because I turned the light on and most other places were dark when we came to your place."

There was no way the poacher happened to be outside his bedroom when Tamala turned on the light. That was too convenient. "The light?" He thought he'd lost them. Especially after he'd gone back outside to hide her obvious yellow truck once Tam was in her room. Who would know which house was his?

"I didn't think about the light. I was so tired I just reacted, but it must have drawn him. I promise you, I didn't call anyone or do anything."

It was too late to worry about that now. He'd heard the poacher's voice and heard him threaten Tamala in person. He'd been knocked too hard to see him clearly, but that would only keep his identity a secret for so long. Clint would figure out where he'd heard that voice before.

As the head ranger, he had to abide by rules, some bigger than others. "Let *us*, the rangers, figure out what to do next. I'd hoped to get you to safety, but now we're down to having you leave with one of the other naturalists tomorrow. I didn't want to have to rely on them, but that is plan C, and definitely the least safe. I want you out of here. This is too dangerous." Fear and anger were tough pills to swallow. He'd failed in keeping her from being attacked again. In his own house.

"I don't want to say I'm scared, but I am. They're still here, even with the snow. They didn't leave. I have nowhere to go. Who will I stay with for two months?" She crossed her arms and scowled out the window. "You told me to hide. That's probably the best plan. We can use the storm to hide. I don't want to risk any of my coworkers getting hurt."

He might not be the perfect man for the job, and he knew there was a hole in his plan. Just because the poacher hadn't known where to look for her after her escape from his room didn't mean he would be gone for long.

No one else in the vicinity was trained to do what Clint did every day. He had to step up and be better. She was finally admitting she needed his help, which meant he couldn't send her off.

He glanced down at the console of Tam's truck. He couldn't do his job as a ranger without a truck and his was out of commission. He probably couldn't do anything other than protect Tamala until she was safe even with a vehicle. They would be stranded within Yellowstone until there was enough snow for his snowmobile and even then, the park service kept the main roads groomed for trucks.

Isolating themselves more would be hard on her. Until they figured out how the poacher kept track of her, they had to assume the poacher was somehow able to track them at all times. "I think we have to put any travel in this truck on hold."

Tam nodded. "But where do we go right now?"

The only place no one else could get into because the interior rooms were one of the safest places in Yellowstone, though it would be the most uncomfortable night she'd ever have. "My office."

SEVEN

Spending the rest of the night in Clint's office seemed like the worst idea he'd ever had, but she realized there was no other choice. Tamala rolled over, her hip throbbing from the cold floor, winding herself deeper into the few blankets Clint had found. The muffled sound of Clint pacing along the hallway kept her awake most of the time anyway, not that her racing thoughts had helped her sleep either.

Every time she closed her eyes, the flash of the poacher's knife blade twisted itself into her memory deeper. That, coupled with the all-too-recent attacks, made sleep impossible. She flailed for a moment until the blankets loosened enough for her to wiggle free. She had too much on her mind for rest anyway.

Outside the door, the aroma of coffee tempted her. The scent opened her senses and made her mouth water. She closed her eyes and sniffed deeply. Coffee helped her ignore the hunger gnawing at her from not eating and the stress of running for her life, at least for a few minutes.

"Morning," she mumbled as she emerged from the closed room.

Clint turned away from his pacing and shot her a guarded smile. "Morning. We made it."

She yawned and hoped she didn't look as tired or frazzled as she felt. She had to think about what had to happen now, the task at hand. Not the fact that a guy who managed to look pretty amazing after a night of no sleep stood in front of her after protecting her all night. Those kinds of thoughts were not welcome when so much rode on her getting either safely out of the park or hidden somewhere within.

"What do we do today?" She went for the small cupboard in the interior interrogation room where they'd stayed and remembered the state of her own destroyed kitchen.

"We have to get the rest of the park workers and any lagging visitors out today. You stick to groups, no matter who suggests you do something else. Stay with other people. Near my team if at all possible. After last night, they'll watch you. No questions asked. Stick with me if you can. But...I got the same feeling you had that I recognized his voice. Be careful who you trust."

She flinched and tried to disregard feeling as if she were betraying her own team and the work they would usually ask her to do. She couldn't do so if she was with the rangers. Naturalists never worked with the rangers. That alone would make people wonder what she was up to and make her more visible. "Are you saying the poacher might be one of our own?"

Clint pressed the warmer button on the coffee maker. "I'm not saying anything for sure yet. I'm only saying the guy's voice was familiar, but he's definitely not someone directly under me. Today we have to make sure the park is clear by the end of the day. My team and I will be out looking for anyone in the park illegally."

She hated team assignments, much preferring to do nature walks as the only guide or doing jobs where she experienced a wildlife environment without the press and voices of others around. But today, team-work sounded like the best plan possible. "What will I be doing while you're chasing any stragglers? That's outside my area."

He pulled out his phone, pressed the screen a few times and frowned. "Not sure. I've had no communica-tion with your team. My phone has almost no connec-tion due to the storm. I'll have to use the satellite phone in my office. I'll watch you and I'll station one of my men near us just in case. If they tell you to pack, you say you're staying in the park under my orders. They may outrank me, but they'll be too distracted with the storm to push further. Help whoever needs it but stick close to me. This guy is afraid to show his face, appar-ently afraid people will recognize him. We'll use that in our favor."

She took a deep breath and shivered. The tempera-ture had dropped as he'd predicted. "How much snow are we looking at?"

He shrugged, then riffled through his mugs, choos-ing one for her. "I'll check the weather radio when we finish here. Last night they warned we only saw the first bit of this storm and the real thing will come on fast this evening then hit in waves over the next few days. But they've had eight hours to update the report and it's been snowing since last night." He poured some coffee in each of the two mugs.

"The primary goal is to stand back and watch carefully. Hopefully, we see those guys leave the park with the potential threat and we can apprehend them. They've got to know the snow might trap them here if this blizzard is as bad as they're predicting. Assuming they're smart enough to have a weather radio with them. I'm not holding out too much hope though."

Poachers planned ahead. They'd have a radio and a strategy in place. With winter hitting early, they would've prepared for a hunt, but probably not for a human target.

If their goal was to silence her and ensure she didn't tell anyone who they were, then they would have dug in and prepared for a long mission. If they trapped her here with no supplies, all the better for them.

She cradled her coffee between her palms. "Is there anywhere in the park to hide a stash of supplies, just in case?" They would be in a hurry. Being trapped in the park meant no way to take out what they shot either. They couldn't be in the park longer than they had to be.

"There are areas, but they're all remote. We haven't kept any buildings secret from you. As a guide, you know where people can go. There are places to hike where people aren't *supposed* to wander, but being in a tent in what's coming wouldn't be comfortable. The cold is survivable with the right gear and heating equipment. The deep snow however…" His brows wove together in thought. "I think they'd have to have more gear than what they could feasibly sneak in."

That limited the poaching team to the back of their Hummer—which wasn't likely—and other bungalows that might be unused. "If they don't leave, how do we find them? I don't want to hide forever, and I don't want to assume they left and be wrong. That mistake might be one of the worst, and last, I ever make."

He took a sip of his coffee, then set the cup down. "The maintenance department will bleed the water lines and shut down most of the concessioner housing for seasonal workers in the off-season. There's no heat or electric to them. If they're staying in one of those places, illegally, they'd freeze without bringing in expensive and bulky equipment. They can't hide all that. The temperature will stay above freezing while the snow is coming down but will drop like a cliff right after. Unless they already have this stuff hiding in the park, it's not coming in."

"It's too much to hope the weather would benefit us."

"I wouldn't count on it. They seem like they're local."

He thought things through before he opened his mouth, which she loved. With the other men who'd briefly come into her life and left, she'd appreciated their looks or their mind, one or the other. Clint had a quick intellect, a good heart and looks that made her struggle to focus on anything else.

The most important factor, though, was he wasn't caving under the pressure. He wasn't passing her off to the nearest sheriff's office or to people she didn't know. The weight of the threats still pressed on her, but he'd lightened the load and he hadn't run off or found someone else to take her when she'd given him the chance.

But would he think less of her if he ever found out she'd doubted him? He was loyal to Yellowstone, she knew that now. But the poachers still had been getting in and getting information somehow, and she'd doubted him at first.

"We'll watch for them today and make a solid plan once we get everyone out of the park."

For the first time since she'd hired on with the park service, one shift seemed like an insurmountable amount of time. "I don't see any other way."

Clint felt Tamala's presence a few feet away the whole day, as if his subconscious had linked to hers somehow. She was there and safe, he knew without turning to look and make himself obvious. Already, members of his fellow law enforcement ranger team had noticed a change in how the naturalists handled teamwork and assignments for the day. Some of his team had given him sidelong and speculative glances. He wasn't supposed to be deciding who stayed where and why.

Let them wonder. He had no time to explain with the blizzard imminent. How could he send her out into the world alone? Because he couldn't leave Yellowstone. The thought made him realize how little he knew about her beyond the park and how much he wanted to fix that.

Naturalist Bonny approached him with a clipboard, her thick mittens clutched tightly to the wood. "I've cleared the visitor's center, sir. I stowed away everything that should be for the off-season and locked the door to guests. The utilities are off." She made a rough check mark on the paper. "Meghan Dale is missing, but her car is still here, in the visitor center lot. No one has heard from her. And Anders Boyce came around to see if we needed help. Haven't seen him in a year."

He got out his own list and checked off what she'd told him. "I wonder what her car is doing there?" He made a note to add that to her file. "And I haven't seen Anders since he left three years ago."

"I told him we had everything under control and that he should head out." She laughed. "He always wanted to help everyone and be everywhere."

"Good work. Thank you for the information on Meghan, I'll follow up with my team and see if we can locate her. You and Tamala can go over to Snow Lodge and help with the lunch prep so you can warm up. I want people in and out as quickly as possible and they're going to need extra hands." He glanced over at Tamala, giving her a nod of approval. "Take Mark with you. Then get your car and get to safety."

He turned and focused on Tamala, hoping she understood his wordless warning to stay inside and close by other people. Bonny was loud enough that he would hear if anything happened.

A huge black truck lurched onto the end of the line where they directed people back out of the park. Clint squinted to get a better view. Was it the Hummer he'd been searching for, or another vehicle? He'd found out quickly lots of people drove big black SUVs. So far, none had been the one they wanted.

Fellow law enforcement ranger Dave tugged his beanie low over his ears against the wind and shivered. "I switched with Jacob. My fingers were freezing. Need to warm up out of the wind for a minute."

He nodded, then followed the seasonal ranger to his office. "Dave? You see anyone today driving a black Hummer, Wyoming plates? Description is in a report from a few days ago. Might have a damaged front bumper." He hadn't ruled out the possibility they'd disguised the damage.

Dave peeled off his mittens and clutched a mug, filling it from the large dispenser on the counter. "Sounds like you've got an exact vehicle in mind. I haven't seen one. They called me to a wildlife incident out past Biscuit Basin. Sedan versus bison. The bison was okay, but we had to call in a tow truck for the car."

That wasn't the direction he'd thought the poachers came from anyway. More likely, the poacher found somewhere for him and his team to stay hidden near Tamala's barracks.

"Thanks. We've had a few reports of the people driving that vehicle causing problems. If you see it parked or driving anywhere in the park, radio me. I want to know. Should be easier to spot the more vehicles leave." The lack of other vehicles would give it away immediately.

He hesitated to call in any of the other section rangers because the threat had stayed so close to Tamala and each ranger covered a vast area, each like their own township, with vast distance between them. He had his own team on the lookout. But the time was right to get all eyes looking for the Hummer and make sure it left the park. He lifted the walkie to his lips.

"Main Office, I need a bulletin sent out to all the Yellowstone areas. If anyone sees a large black Hummer with Wyoming plates, I want to know immediately."

The crackling response came back almost immediately. "Clint, this is Jared over at Canyon. I found a truck matching the description of the vehicle you're looking for parked at the Mary Mountain trailhead in Hayden Valley. Looks abandoned. Over."

Hayden Valley was an hour's drive from Old Faithful and nowhere near where they'd been last night. His chest tightened. He hadn't seen the truck yesterday, only the one poacher. If they weren't in the truck, easily distinguishable, then they could be anywhere, driving anything, and he had no way to track them.

"I'll be there as soon as I can." He tossed on his hat, grabbed a flashlight, and motioned for Dave to hand over his keys.

He nodded and pulled them from his coat pocket. "Just make sure it gets back to me with all the windows."

He hated that he couldn't make any guarantees. At least if the poachers were following him, he'd be leading them away from Tam. She was safe in the cafeteria, surrounded by at least five other people and his second in command. Any of those men would have to be fools to try something there.

An hour later, as he pulled into the small parking area, he saw the vehicle they'd been looking for. The vicinity was empty. Jared peered around from the other side. "I've circled around in search of the owner, radioed others, and no one has seen anyone near here. Seems like they dumped it."

How had he missed those conversations? He'd focused too much on Tamala and what he needed to do to get the park clear. He'd been concentrating on looking for that specific truck, instead of paying attention to the radio traffic which might've led him to answers. "Anything else lead you to believe the truck is abandoned and not just waiting?"

"The flat front tire." Jared hunkered down on the other side to inspect it. "Looks like it was in some kind of accident. The bumper is scuffed."

So, had one of his shots hit the Hummer or had the sharp undercarriage from hitting his truck popped it? No way to know. The poachers had to have another vehicle with them, and Clint would never know if they'd left the park.

"This was the vehicle the shooters were in. Is it unlocked? Any licenses or insurance inside so we can call it in?" Maybe they would finally see a break in the case if there was insurance registered to a real name.

"No. Didn't look into the truck that much. I was more interested in finding the owner and offering to help get them out of here. I'm sorry I didn't call in to check the plate. I was just focused on getting people out." Jared's walkie crackled, and he turned away. A moment later he turned back. "I need to get back to Canyon."

"Go. I won't be here long. Thanks for your help." He couldn't really blame Jared for assuming the vehicle was like any other, possibly belonging to people who were temporarily lost. But now they had it and they could have it examined.

He didn't want to be there if the owner of the truck returned, especially since the poacher likely wouldn't be alone. Even with training, he didn't want to put himself in a situation where he was outnumbered. Gun or not, that wasn't a fight he'd walk into.

He glanced at the vast area of Hayden Valley. Dark clouds spread out over the sky. The Mary Mountain trail led up an incline for miles off the Grand Loop Road. An ambitious hiker could cover the entire trail and end up on the other side of the park—his district—in about thirteen hours. The only way to do that was to leave a vehicle at the other trailhead.

. Had these guys really abandoned their vehicle, hiked all day, and met someone to pick them up on the other side? Someone who had a car close by…like Meghan? He shook the thought away. She'd given Tamala the advice to leave, but that could've been for her benefit, to put him off her track. He'd have Mark dig through Meghan's file when he returned.

Hiking that trail required great stamina and preparation, especially in the snow. There were no backcountry campsites. Camping overnight on Mary Mountain was illegal, not that a poacher would bother following rules.

Some people went off those marked areas at risk of injury. Some didn't care. He doubted any of the men chasing Tamala were there for the scenery. They probably weren't anywhere near the abandoned vehicle. They left it there to make Tamala squirm, and probably as an open threat to him.

All four doors of the Hummer were locked. In the back, with the heavily tinted windows and black leather seats, he saw a box of garbage bags, electrical tape and rope. He moved to the front seat and, in plain view, there were two maps lying out. One folded, but heavily used with the state of Wyoming on the front. The other was a Yellowstone handbook, easily accessible from the gift shop. Someone had penned in the various barracks, and there were Xs over the visitor's center and Tamala's house.

He pounded the window once out of frustration and headed back for his truck to radio the Yellowstone seasonal law enforcement team in the Mammoth Hot Springs section. They were the head, and they needed to know there was a threatening vehicle in the park, even if they sent the Canyon Village wrecker to get it.

He'd talk to people he trusted and tell them what little he knew, because this went well beyond what his team, alone, could handle.

When they towed the truck, he'd tell them his suspicions about the items in the back seat. That, in addition to his and Tamala's statements, would add to the case against these men. There had to be prints in the truck. They had used it to assault him and Tamala, there might even be evidence inside from shooting at them on the road.

He'd tell Tamala the Hummer was locked up tight and out of play, but he'd keep the information about what was in the back seat to himself, because she already knew they were after her life; the evidence would only terrify her more. That, along with the feelings growing inside him for Tamala.

He was getting good at keeping those under wraps.

EIGHT

Tamala watched from a small crowd inside the Snow Lodge as the last visitor drove toward the exit. The nearest town big enough to have a hotel for them was forty miles away in Mammoth Hot Springs. On slow roads, the drive would take well over two hours, and those hotels would remain open after November first.

Mark clapped her on the back, sending her tumbling forward. "Where are you headed? Got yourself all packed?"

He only asked to make small talk, but she didn't have an answer. Clint hadn't given her any clue as to what she should say beyond, "staying with him and not leaving the park." He'd been working with others, though near her, most of the day, and they hadn't talked since their morning coffee.

As the head ranger of the Old Faithful section, Clint had to stay on-site year-round, winter season or not. The park would start preparing the roads for oversnow travel once there was a good snowpack, then they'd open the gates for snowmobile and snow coach tours. A huge plow crew would tackle snow removal on the roads right around Easter, and that's when she'd normally return. But this year was different. It had to be.

"I have a few things to do yet," she evaded, hoping he asked nothing further.

He rubbed his hands together to warm them, then saluted her, though he technically outranked her in the chain of command.

"Have a good winter break. See you back in March." His eyebrows rose as if he'd asked a question.

Her nerves hummed. Why was he asking? His voice didn't match the poacher nor the men who'd ransacked her cabin, but could he be connected? Was he a plant to make her give up information? She certainly didn't want them to know even more than they already did. "I'm sure I'll have everything ready to go in time and I'll see you then." She waved in return then turned away to evade any other questions.

Clint drove up in Dave's pickup, climbed out and slammed the door. His dark brown coat covered much of his uniform, but his ranger hat set him above the others. He took a quick appraising glance around and made eye contact with her, sending a little jolt through her, before he nodded his approval. She realized she hadn't felt as safe with him gone.

"Excellent work, everyone. Get your gear packed and get yourselves safely out of the way of this storm."

Clint had to answer to the park service, and she still wasn't certain he'd allow her to stay against their rules. She felt safest with him. If the poachers left to avoid the snow, she would hide somewhere with Clint until the roads opened up to oversnow travel. Yellowstone gave no exceptions. Ever. So he'd either have to tell them he'd broken the rules and risk losing the job he loved, or keep it a secret that he'd let Tamala stay.

Clint stopped to talk to a few people. She didn't want to speak with anyone and say something wrong that would get Clint in trouble, so she hung back slightly. He already faced a report and possible write-up because of her if she stayed. As Bonny turned toward her, he made his way over.

"I think it's time we go take care of your bungalow before dark sets in and there's no time left." He glanced to the sky as the flurries intensified, skittering around in the driving wind.

Bonny gasped, her eyes wide. "You haven't packed yet? Oh, Tam, do you need my help? The roads are so bad, and they'll only get worse. It'll take hours to get anywhere."

Her friend was far too sweet and would be terrified by the state of her bungalow. "No, it's fine. I've got almost all I need."

He nodded his agreement and faced Bonny. "Thanks for offering, but I'd feel better if you packed your car and got on the road. Send me a message to let me know you got somewhere safe tonight."

Bonny frowned and glanced between the two of them. "I will. There's a hotel room waiting for me in Mammoth. If you don't have a room yet, you can stay with me, Tam. Ask at the front desk when you get there."

Bonny smiled and gave her an enormous hug, then headed off toward her housing unit.

"What are we going to do from here?" she asked Clint and licked her cracked lips. "I know they didn't leave today. You would've said something if they had."

The fact that he hadn't set off alarm bells. "Unless there's something important you want to tell me?"

Clint glanced around the parking area just outside the Snow Lodge, biding his time and formulating the right words. There were a lot of things he wanted to tell her. All of them he probably *should* tell her. But she'd been through enough and adding to her burden of worry wouldn't make her more watchful, it would only add stress.

"You're right. They're still in the park as far as I know." First, the wrecker crew has to finish the tow, then examine the inside of the truck.

He didn't want to think about losing her or that there were only two choices: she had to break the rules and stay, or he had to break the rules, lose his job and leave the park to take her somewhere. The park was his domain, his first love. Without him, he would leave it unprotected. *Lord, what do I do?* A 3472-square mile area—over two million acres—of federally protected land was his life's work. But there was only one Tamala Roth. Would the park service understand if she stayed?

"What are your thoughts?" He'd appreciated her ability to form a good plan before, and perhaps he'd looked too far into her case without asking.

"I don't want to run anymore. We've been running for four straight days. The poachers have the upper hand, and I don't like feeling this all-encompassing fear. I think we should decide where we're going to be and stand our ground or both leave."

If defending a position was possible, he would. But if he left Yellowstone, his job was finished. Letting her leave alone relieved him of duty but killed his honor and made his chest constrict.

"I can't leave." He had to give her credit for valor. He was tired of running, but they had no way to defend themselves when they didn't know where the battle might come from.

"Standing our ground sounds like a good plan, except we know they have at least two guns—the shotgun he used the first day and the handgun he used on your truck—plus one very long knife. We've got my service pistol, bear spray and kitchen utensils along with a few rifles, which aren't great for concealing."

His other guns were back at his cabin and definitely not as dependable as the one on his hip. He'd gone back that morning to make sure he'd locked up after they'd abandoned his place. Even with the screen off and the window wide open, nothing had gone inside except a snow drift and nothing else went missing.

The poacher left no sign he'd returned there after he'd escaped. Which meant he was only on the hunt for Tamala. He could've returned and made a disaster of Clint's home, but he hadn't done a thing besides hit Clint and run after Tamala. At least she'd sprinted away fast enough.

"Then what would you propose?" She stood stiffly and pressed her thumbs to her back as she stretched, then yawned. He'd listened to her shifting all night. She had slept little the night before, only slightly more than he had.

What was the best choice that would keep them both alive and catch an attempted murderer? "I think we need to keep on the lookout for anyone around the Old Faithful area. They are focused on you. For now, we'll stay here. If they show up, they'll stick out. If this snow gets as deep as the meteorologists think and the park service gives the okay, we'll use the snowmobiles. We'll stay in Meghan's cabin since there's room, and it's near my stored food."

"At Meghan's?" Her eyes widened, and she stared at him. "Won't they shut off the electricity?"

He laughed, finally releasing some of the tension he'd held on to all day. "Yes, it won't be comfortable, but the poachers won't expect it. And, since you know her better, maybe you'll see something my men missed when they looked through her bungalow."

She nodded her agreement as her glance darted around them. Snow already blanketed everything. "Then that sounds like a good plan."

Tamala was perfect. She was an intelligent outdoorswoman who happened to be the most beautiful woman he'd ever seen. She had faith and strength. But just because she was perfect for him didn't mean he had the option to fall in love. His life's work was still as a law enforcement ranger and he wasn't ready. Not after the loss of his wife.

"We need to get settled in soon to weather this storm." She took a deep breath. "Do you think they'll see us?"

"There's less chance if we go now when there's no one around. But they've followed us everywhere else."

He hated the feeling of loss her words generated. "I think you're right. We should use the rest of today when they are hunkered down to make sure no one is around Meghan's place." And that's what it would take without knowing their mode of transportation.

That Hummer hadn't been big enough to hold an ATV, but if they'd brought in illegal snowmobiles on a trailer with a vehicle that already left, they had free rein. There was no other way to get the equipment in. *If* that was true, their group might be smaller now.

"I agree. Let's grab some skis to get to our destination and dig in. The tracks might keep them guessing, too." She headed for the Snow Lodge to get her laptop.

They had to remain unseen until they were sure they could face the poachers and survive. Or making a stand might be the last thing they did.

NINE

Tamala tried to focus on the park's beauty, but the blowing snow pelting her helmet made enjoyment almost impossible. To prevent getting lost, and ending up where they shouldn't and remaining mostly hidden, they were using cross-country skis. This also meant she had to keep up with the rope around Clint's waist as he cut a path through the thick snow toward Meghan's cabin. At least they couldn't be seen. She could barely see Clint a few feet in front of her.

Clint stopped and cleared his goggles, then pointed to an area along the low, heavily treed ridgeline. With minimal visibility, she barely made out the dark outline of the evergreens.

Tamala hurried to keep up as Clint skied toward their new home base. The closer they got, the easier it was to see buildings and landmarks. The remains of a tent flapped in the wind near the Old Faithful cabins. Bright fabric stood out against all the white anchored over the top of the tent. The entire structure waved precariously, as if it hadn't been set up well or had been there a long time. Either option was feasible.

Clint stopped far enough away to remain cautious. He flipped up his tinted goggles to look around, and she did the same. Immediately, the wind hit her in the face and her lungs burned with the cold. She held her breath until she turned her head away from the blast.

With slow ease, Clint unlatched his skis and lowered to his knees behind an outcropping to hide. She followed his lead.

"Hard to tell from this distance, but I don't think anyone is in there the way it's bouncing around in the wind. Not enough weight inside to secure it down. I think it's pretty safe to approach."

She had to agree, but was this a trap or just someone who left in a hurry? The four corners were anchored, but not well, and the tent looked like it might blow away any moment.

"Should we get closer and look? Maybe an illegal camper left behind their garbage if the tent ripped?" Campers who stayed in an area they shouldn't didn't care about leaving trash behind.

She hoped that's all this was, so she wouldn't see where her attackers had slept. If they didn't sleep, in her mind they were less human. The rangers and naturalists were forever picking up after campers who'd left items behind. Just because they found a tent out of place didn't mean those particular people left it behind.

"I think we're safe to draw in closer. Let's not hike until we have to. Conserve energy and use the skis. If it didn't look empty, I wouldn't."

She flipped down her goggles and gave him a thumbs-up so he knew she agreed, then strapped her skis back on and took in a deep breath of cold air as she shoved off. No matter how she tried to talk herself out of the fear of the tent and what they might find inside, the panic held fast. The poachers were still in her park. Somewhere. If not the owners of the tent, then somewhere close.

Without Clint, she'd have had to do this all on her own. She wouldn't have been able to get his opinion. She would be out looking for a safe place to hide by herself, and also hiding from Clint in his section of the park. A section he knew better than her.

He stopped alongside the back of the flapping orange fabric, unzipped his snowsuit, and drew his pistol. It seemed obvious there was no one inside. The door slapped in the gusty wind and though the snow fell opposite the open door, a drift had blown inside, which was the only thing keeping the tent from blowing away.

"I'm going around and in first. Wait for the all-clear." He met her gaze and even through the distortion of the snow and goggles, her stomach flipped.

Nerves. Just nerves. Of course she was nervous, not noticing how much he seemed to care or how his eyes warmed when they landed on her. No, that was his job.

He ducked inside, and called to her a moment later.

Tamala crouched in the door and found a small leather satchel near the entrance. She tugged off her mittens and the biting cold made them almost instantly red and prickly.

"Look at this!" she called over the wind.

Clint came over to where she knelt and tugged his goggles and gloves off. They were out of the wind, but not warm. He unzipped the sack and reached inside. There were food wrappers, receipts, a Yellowstone parking pass, a pair of plastic gloves and a towel that looked bloody. She reached for them and stopped as he pulled it back.

"This was theirs." He shoved everything into the bag and zipped it shut, avoiding her gaze.

"How do you know?" The chill running up her spine wasn't from the cold. He'd never sounded like that before. What told him those receipts were theirs? They had no names, even if they signed the bottom which would be a rookie mistake for anyone hiding out.

He took a deep breath and moved some of the drifted snow with his boot. "I didn't tell you earlier, but one guy from my team found the Hummer. I saw items in the back. The receipt in here is for some of those items. There were a few different things, but one of them was a map of Yellowstone with your cabin marked."

This *had* been their tent, no question about it. They might still be nearby. "So, they were here, but most likely aren't coming back. They've left their garbage all over Yellowstone. We've got what they left—let's get going."

She hated litter and the casual way some people left things around. This was different though, like they wanted her to find their castoffs and know they were still after her. A bright orange tent was a challenge to her, like a flag. But why leave the receipts and rag?

"Are you going to show me what else they had in the back of that Hummer?"

"I don't have it. Everything was locked in the back and the vehicle wasn't opened until the wrecker team got it to Mammoth. This will be added to the stack of evidence against them. Our word will only go so far."

"What's our next step?"

He glanced at the floor one last time, then met her eyes. "They're leaving clues. Maybe there's more in the bag if we examine the contents. We'll bring this back to Meghan's and search through everything piece by piece. I'll call Mark and ask if the Mammoth team found any more marks on the map in the front seat of the Hummer or any other evidence like prints."

"That's good. The more evidence against them, the better. I'm just worried about the guys at Mammoth knowing, since we don't know who the guy on the inside is."

"I know what you mean, but I trust the Mammoth team. They're the ones who'll take this guy to jail." His face was unreadable. She trusted him, more than she thought she ever could.

She had to be totally up-front and tell him all she knew. Every bit. "When I told Meghan about the attack, she said something that's been eating at me. She knew… everything. Before I told her. Gossip is rampant, but usually not so accurate. I'd heard rumors, too. Rumors of poachers within the ranks in Yellowstone. What if our guy is connected to someone in Mammoth or Hot Springs? Or right here in Old Faithful?" She swallowed hard, waiting for him to be offended and walk away. She would be. Her own team was like family, all the more for the law enforcement rangers.

"I appreciate that you trust me, and maybe me alone. I won't break that trust. I had the same worries about you at first. I'm still worried about Meghan and that she hasn't turned up. I can promise you that none of the men I work with are associated with poachers. That doesn't mean you're wrong. He's way too familiar with Yellowstone. Maybe we should be looking at the lists of concessioners and other seasonal workers, too." He tucked the satchel in his coat and zipped it shut, then patted where it was hidden to make sure it would stay put. "Let's head to Meghan's where we can talk easier," he said as he tugged his gloves back on.

Why hadn't she thought of the concessioners? They weren't hired by the park service, but by outside vendors. They were the perfect group for the poachers to use since they could get in the park, but weren't really connected to it.

She bundled back up, but before either of them went for their skis, it seemed understood that they would take down the tent and bring it with them. They picked up the tent to avoid letting it blow away and hurt any wildlife. Since Clint already carried her bag, she rolled up the tent and stuck it through the rope already around her waist.

The trail they'd laid on the way had already blown over, and the drifts were about two feet deep after five hours of hard snowfall. Dense cloud cover and thick snow obliterated visibility. Clint slowed his pace and seemed lost for a few moments. Everything around looked white, and the usually visible low ridgeline and other landmarks lay hidden behind the squall. Twilight stalked them, and conditions would soon be impossible to navigate the short distance off the trail where they were. Clint pulled up his sleeve to look at his watch and slowly turned to get his bearings.

First, she heard a quiet *pop*, then slicing pain cut through her hip, severing the six foot length of rope connecting her to Clint. She froze as pain burned down her leg and the rope flapped for a moment in the wind behind Clint. He continued forward likely unaware of the danger.

She reached out, catching the end of the rope. If he got too far away, she'd never find him again. Something hit her from behind and slicing pain drove her to the ground. She held on for dear life as her arm seemed to weaken by the second.

He dragged her for a few moments, then her grip slipped. She forced herself to ignore the pain and try to see anything around her. The tent strapped to her back slapped in the wind, hitting her as her concentration faltered. Only then did she realize the bright orange tent had to have been what the poacher saw.

Where had Clint gone? She wouldn't move so he could retrace his steps before they disappeared. He had to be using the trail as a lifeline to find her, but that meant the poacher could, too. Clint reached her and kneeled by her side. "What happened?"

She barely heard him over the wind.

Another muffled *ping* and Clint covered her with his body. "Hang on, Tam!"

She hardly heard him through all the layers of hats and hoods. Though he was only inches from her ear, he seemed far away.

The distant security lights of the Old Faithful Inn flickered through the storm. She tried to focus on doing as she was told and not let her mind wander, but the pain seemed to ramp up quickly and her hip throbbed hot in the freezing night. She opened her mouth to tell

him she didn't have the strength to hold on when another man appeared out of the storm.

Hold on, Tam... Clint prayed Tamala wouldn't let
go. *Lord, I need the strength of a lion right now. You
said I can do all things through Christ who strength-
ens me, I need that...* A man kept pace with them and
even pushed ahead, forcing Clint to think ahead. How
could he get away?

Clint gripped Tamala's arm tightly, her weight both
heavy and totally welcome. He'd thought he'd lost her a
moment before. Racing as fast as his legs would carry
him, he tried to veer off so the man couldn't see them.
The wind and snow were his only hope to hide. Once
he put enough distance between them and the poacher,
he could check his location.

Tamala needed him to get to a place where he could
examine her wound and hide. His mind flew with possibilities since Meghan's was now too far away for comfort. They were close to the Old Faithful Inn, but there
was no way to heat such a large building once the power
inside was off and nowhere for them to hide inside. He'd
also have to find some way to get her medical attention if her wound was more than he could handle on his
own. Not an easy thing to do when they were stranded
in Yellowstone in a blizzard.

The medical clinic was close by, but locked. He had
the key, but did he have time? He heard another slight
pop, and a hole appeared in a tree trunk close to his left.
This was exactly why he hadn't wanted to go back to
his barracks or to Tamala's. He was outgunned and out
of time. If Clint didn't lose this guy in the storm, they

would be caught. Outside, in a blizzard, alone with a man they knew had excellent aim.

Tamala gripped the back of his coat for a moment, then let go. He felt her weight shift as she tumbled into the snow. His heart slammed as he stopped in place and cranked around to see where she'd landed. The other man skied by them, about fifteen yards distant. Clint heard the steady slide and *clop* of the skis as the poacher turned around to come back.

Clint released his skis and retraced his path a few steps. Barely visibly, he found a dark mound of fabric a few yards back, the tent was hidden underneath her. The other man closed in on him as he gripped the back of Tamala's coat. Another shot ripped his coat and adrenaline coursed through him, making him think faster.

He hit the ground and swung his arm through the bank beside them, making a tiny avalanche of snow to cover them enough to hide. With as little movement as possible, he checked his watch compass. Old Faithful was in the wrong direction, and the man came closer and closer, the crunch of the snow sounding loud with nothing but wind around him.

The other man raced alongside. Clint waited what felt like an eternity to put space between him and the poacher, then pushed away from the snowbank. Tamala rolled her head slightly, coming to. He gripped her arm to help her stand but held tight. His heart twisted when he saw the pain in her eyes. He had to get far enough ahead of the other man to take Tamala inside without their assailant seeing him.

He held back his pace because of visibility and Tam's

fatigue. If he wasn't careful, he'd go where he didn't want to—like a hot spring.

The noise of the other skier was lost in the storm, and he let himself slow down as he stopped on a flat plain away from any tree coverage, at least as far as visibility allowed him to see. In the distance, the lights of the inn flickered. But what lay between them? Immediately, he felt far too exposed. Swiveling to see, he lost his balance.

He gripped tight to Tamala as they lurched forward in a tangle of legs and arms. Where had the man gone and would he be back? This was not the end. Tam needed him, she was hurt, and he refused to let her attacker get her now. Waiting for someone to appear out of the snow forced his senses to heightened alert. He heard the snowflakes as they hit the ground.

Without light, he had no way to see where the poacher went or which direction they faced. With a loud crack and flash, a power pole arced in the direction he needed to go.

The only way to break free was to force their attackers to lose themselves in the storm. He had to disappear, or Tam would never make it. They hadn't seen him in the drift and he had to make the call—should he stay and risk Tamala losing too much blood or run and risk capture?

He held tight to Tam and shoved snow over them to hide. Soon they'd be invisible, but he'd also be stuck out in a freezing blizzard with an injured woman. And no way to tell how far he needed to carry her or when he'd be safe to move.

The buzz of fear filled his head as he gripped tight to Tamala and plunged deeper into the drift, a prayer for his life and hers coursing through him.

TEN

The abrupt cold snow down Tamala's neck forced her awake. Then the jarring of her hip as Clint shifted her in the snow took her breath away. She tried to curl into a ball for protection. Clinging to her stomach, she prayed for safety as Clint's arms surrounded her.

"Just be still for a minute. The snow is wet and thick enough that he won't be able to see us down here unless he skis right into us." Clint's reassuring voice in her ear calmed her.

She tried to nod and realized he probably lay too close to see her. Maybe he'd felt her head move. Every second that ticked by lying there in his arms helped relieve the fear ratcheting through her after she'd been shot.

After what seemed like an hour, Clint whispered, "I think we've waited long enough for him to lose us. Come on. Go as fast you can. We have to get somewhere safe."

He unhooked the tent from her back. "He can't track us without this. I think that's how he found us. Since I lost them back where we hid first, I'll come back later for our skis and the tent."

Fast. She could probably do that. Had to. With Clint's

help, she pushed to her feet and pressed forward, each step painful and dizzying. Someone moved in the distance, like a circling vulture waiting for the right moment, or was that just the snow, confusing her mind?

Nearby, car lights splashed through the driving snow, right at them. Clint covered his face against the bright light, and she prayed whoever it was worked for the park.

The vibration of the nearby engine tingled over her skin, and she closed her eyes. Gauging distance, where she was, or what road could be there, proved impossible. They might be in the middle of a highway. He could drive right over them in the dark swirling blizzard. If the killer found them, he'd probably shoot them both.

The car slowly drove toward them and Tamala prayed for them to go around, to veer off in another direction. The rumble got closer until the hum filled her whole body. A blast of snow knocked against her and swirled around them, preventing her from seeing anything as the car slowly passed by, then drove away.

"We don't have time to count this as a victory. They'll be back."

Tamala flinched because he had to yell to be heard, yet everything in her wanted to be silent and avoid anyone knowing they were there. Scorching pain burned through her as she scanned around them. Where were they?

They were way off-course and nothing around them seemed familiar. Snow blanketed every surface, and the swirling flakes obscured her vision more than a few feet ahead. Her hip throbbed in protest, not wanting to hold her weight, as she tried to find solid footing in the deep snow.

Clint peeled back his sleeve and pressed a button on his watch. A compass appeared, and he turned their direction then kept them at a steady pace. The heavy deep snow slowed her down, but the urgency to find somewhere safe kept her moving.

In the distance, a tall security light appeared. The beam of light gave her hope they would find a safe place soon. Her leg was freezing, and she suspected a bullet had torn through her snowsuit and grazed her. They'd be able to at least get out of the snow, though none of the rental cabins had any place to start a fire or cook that wasn't outside.

They reached one of the small Old Faithful Inn cabins, and Clint managed to break into the first one. As soon as he closed the door, he plucked off her goggles and her head spun. He sat her down in the nearest chair and stripped his coat off.

"You'll freeze," she chattered, feeling like she might curl up and turn into an icicle herself.

He didn't listen and helped her out of her mittens and coat, then out of her snow pants. A bright swath of red covered her outer thigh, and her pants were ragged and torn, hanging slightly open to reveal a gash.

"It's as clean as we could hope." He glanced around the room, but the cabin held relatively little. There was a sink in a tiny alcove in the corner, the bathroom was more like a closet and one bed sat in the middle taking up most of the space. The small room held few comforts and definitely no medical supplies.

"Will you need to amputate, doc?" she joked, trying to find some levity in the situation.

"I'm sure you'll live." He dug in a huge pocket in the thigh of his cargo pants and pulled out a sealed roll of bandage wrap. "I know this won't fix the gash, but it'll stop the bleeding until we can get back to the clinic for supplies. Thank God it only grazed you."

She slowly nodded her understanding. As the law enforcement ranger, he was almost as qualified as the RN who worked in the medical building. She really was in expert hands.

After he settled her in, she pictured right where they were in relation to Old Faithful. Returning to Yellowstone housing created a hazardous situation with the blizzard. Staying could be deadly. If their attacker or one of his lackeys saw Clint and Tamala go inside, they might follow. If they didn't, Clint and Tamala had more pressing issues. "We aren't too far from Meghan's. If we stay here, we'll freeze."

"If we leave, we freeze. At least here, we can do some basic things to stay warm. There are a few blankets on the bed, we've still got our snow gear, even if it's wet."

He quickly wrapped her leg around her cotton pants. "I'm not having you get colder and waste energy to take them off. For now, this will work."

He left her to bundle back in her coat as he maneuvered the mattress off the bed into a saggy tent, laying down the desk chair next to the bed to support the far end. "We'll use this as a dense layer, then we'll wrap in the blankets underneath, trapping as much heat as we can from our bodies."

She shivered, thinking about how cold the floor

probably was. Her hands shook as she climbed into his fort and sat against the wooden base of the standard hotel bed.

"We won't sweat, that's for sure, but the proximity of our bodies will create the heat needed to survive." He lifted the mattress and tucked three blankets over her. He climbed in next to her and pulled them over himself.

His matter-of-fact statement took away all her unease. Tamala laid her head against the mattress and closed her eyes. Not that the discomfort mattered; the dim light coming through the windows wasn't enough to bother her tired eyes, but she couldn't bring herself to sleep.

"You did great out there. Not many people can get shot at and handle themselves like you."

"Thanks." She opened her eyes, and his handsome face was mere inches away. Surprisingly, in the dark she knew every one of his features.

Her job had been dangerous, but no one had ever said she might be at the wrong end of a gun. If she'd had to cope with this situation alone, she wouldn't have survived. The feeling of being utterly lost in the snow and a bullet wound, even if it was just a graze, were too much.

Clint had made sure she survived. He'd come back and rescued her when he could've skied away for safety and help. He didn't have to push her to be her best, but he did. She leaned forward, wanting the kiss she only sought from him, then stalled. What if he wasn't thinking the same way she was? What if he didn't need her at all?

He leaned in and met her lips, rocking her to her toes. His slow attention stilled her entire body until she could focus on nothing else. When he parted from her and silence pulsed between them, it asked questions she wasn't sure how to answer.

No one had gotten to him the way Tamala did. Maybe her kiss wouldn't have been half as sweet if he didn't think she was amazing to begin with, but there was no way to test his theory. He already wanted to kiss her again.

Now, hours later, thoughts of her kept him awake. He had to keep her out of reach, but how, now that he had no skis and the snow buried every vehicle by at least a couple feet? The roads wouldn't be cleared for days. They'd only had the first leg of the blizzard. More snow was on the way. Leaving wasn't an option.

They'd taken turns sleeping wrapped in their snow gear and blankets. Their body heat kept the small tent tolerable, but the floor was uncomfortable no matter what.

She wasn't right for him. Especially now, in the middle of a crisis. Yet she was perfect, too. He watched her sleep, giving her longer to rest than he took, mostly because she actually slept. After her injury, she needed to recuperate.

Though the blizzard hemmed them in, they'd relied on a small emergency lantern someone had left behind in the bedside table. The light wasn't much, but the narrow glow helped chase away the shadows. He'd tested the little heater in the room, and as he'd suspected, it hadn't worked.

After he'd finished checking the door, he reminded himself he'd need to get ahold of the hospitality company who owned the cabins to let them know what happened and pay for the damage. Outside, the first silvery light of morning strained through the crystalline covered windows. The snow had slowed, but the reprieve wouldn't last long. If they didn't get to Meghan's or his office now, they might not get another chance.

His stomach protested any movement at all that didn't take him to food. Hopefully there would be something in her cabin they could make. They hadn't eaten in over a day and he needed at least an hour of actual sleep and something in his belly. But would they be able to walk back to housing and radio for help without finding the poachers?

Since they had limited time, he woke Tamala and cleaned up the survival fort. "It's getting light outside. We should use this time to get where we need to be before the storm starts again and while the few people left in Yellowstone are out and moving. Just being there will provide cover for us."

She nodded and stretched her uninjured leg with a stiff yawn. "I'll be happy to get back where it's warm."

He held the door open for her.

"Thanks." She yawned and looked both ways before she left the little cabin. "I feel like I don't belong outside, or anywhere."

"I know what you mean. Every time we show our faces, he appears out of nowhere to drive us back in."

Clint stewed over whether he should mention what had happened between them, but she wasn't acting any differently. Had he fallen into a trap, allowing a woman to pull his heartstrings? Had emotion overwhelmed her to make her kiss him? Was his heart ready for someone else?

He walked quickly, keeping his eyes and ears open for anyone. Tamala appeared to be doing the same as her head swiveled back and forth. The park was eerily quiet and white everywhere.

"With all this snow, we won't have use of a truck anymore, so they can't drive either. I wonder if they left in that car? Last night was brutal. If they didn't have anywhere to hide and find warmth and shelter, we might be looking for bodies." She gave an exaggerated shiver.

He didn't want to follow along that line of thinking yet. If they found the poaching ring and brought them to justice, that would be better than death. "I should follow up with the Mammoth team and see if they found anything in the Hummer. Let's go to my office where I know there's food and working communications."

"I trust your judgment." She tensed next to him.

"I think you and I need to find some backup. We're facing odds I can't match, especially since they have weapons. Nothing about this situation is in our favor."

"Except with all this snow, who could we possibly call?"

He could trust his team and they would come as soon as possible. He'd known those people for years, and they looked out for each other. "The other law enforcement rangers might have information about poachers in their areas that we don't."

"You should've gone through the Hummer before you turned it over."

She wasn't acting as if anything about them had changed. She almost seemed colder toward him. Maybe kissing him had made her realize they were wrong for each other. He'd lost himself in false hope. He'd thought they had something when what they had was a stressful situation. Stress either shoved people together or apart. He should know that by now.

"I don't have the tools or the inclination to break into vehicles." Though he'd been tempted when he'd seen the map with the X over her house.

"You still have the satchel. I saw it at the cabin when you took off your gear. That will have to do."

"We can do that after lunch. Then we need to decide what to do next. No more running off."

She nodded and went in the moment he'd unlocked the door to his office. He didn't blame her. Being outside had to grate on her nerves after the last few days. He turned up the heat higher than he would normally allow. Without thinking any further ahead than he needed to, he tugged some chicken from the office refrigerator and handed it to her. "I'll take first watch so you can get some rest, then we'll switch. Until we form a plan, I've got to go talk to Mark. You can take the couch."

He reached for her to give her a brief embrace and she held up her hand for him to stop.

"I'm sorry, it's nothing. I'm just tired." She didn't touch him. Her chilly reaction seemed to indicate she wanted to avoid contact with him at all.

"Just tired," he repeated, taking a step back.

If Tamala had regrets about their kiss, he wouldn't push a response from her. Especially when he was sure he was the wrong guy for a relationship. "Then I'll let you get some rest," he said as he backed into the hall, feeling like a criminal for reaching out.

"It's no big deal." Tamala tried to smile but failed. "I'm going to grab a little food, go take a nap and then unwrap this bandage and take a look, see if I'll need stitches or anything." She gently rubbed her bandaged leg.

Someone other than him should look at it, though he was the only medically trained person there. Every word felt so distant and cold. The way it should be, but his heart said it was all wrong.

He vowed there would be no more kissing or closeness. He had to stop himself from getting any nearer and losing his heart.

He leaned against the wall near the window where he could see anyone trying to get near the office. At least he could do that much for Tam, if nothing else.

ELEVEN

This can't be happening. She wasn't supposed to be falling for Clint when she should be focused on staying alive.

Tamala curled under the blankets and tugged them up to her chin, unable to sleep. She closed her eyes, thinking about his kiss and what it might mean. No matter how much she'd enjoyed it, now wasn't the time to look deeper. Her heart hated to let those few minutes go, but survival had to come first.

She had too much at stake for her to think about him as more than her protector and a law enforcement ranger. All the teasing and taunting she'd heard in high school and college filled her memories. Smart girls didn't marry great guys.

If she survived this…Clint would be in Yellowstone next year, and she would have to face him if she wanted to work here.

That was all cart before the horse thinking. She had to survive first before she worried about next year. If their kiss was only a onetime thing, she would hold on to that feeling as important. Probably for years to come. Guys like him weren't everywhere.

Romantic encounters in her life had been limited to first dates and awkward social setups by friends. Guys never wanted another date after they realized she loved science and wasn't about to put her passion for research on hold for a relationship. Though she wouldn't have to put off her love of the wilderness with Clint; he would challenge her to do even more for the causes she loved.

Images of snow drifts, racing through the storm, flashing lights and excruciating pain wouldn't let her sleep. Had the adrenaline pushed her to Clint? He'd been her rock all day long, faithfully sticking with her. If the Lord had sent her a guide, Clint had done the job.

Through the entire day, full of highs and lows, Clint had been calm. He'd taken care of her and himself. He'd planned and executed everything. Those abilities had drawn her to him. Not just a handsome face, but a mind and heart matched by none. Scientifically, he was perfect for her.

She punched the throw pillow softly and listened for any sound from the next room. There was a science to attraction, but what she'd done had defied reason. To become involved with the man who protected her was foolish. She had diverted his attention from his job.

Unable to sleep, she sat up and took her time unwinding the tape covering her leg. She hadn't wanted to, but it gave her something to think about. Even when she'd been injured, he'd been prepared. He'd had bandages in his pocket. She hadn't considered they might need first aid. Her only concern had been to get somewhere safe.

The gash was angry and pink under the bandage. She went to the bathroom and gently washed the area, put on some antiseptic from the med kit on the shelf, then took a better look. The gash the bullet left wasn't deep and, as Clint had said, the wound was about as clean as possible. Whichever of the poachers had been chasing them, had missed.

The wound had bled enough to scare her, and she still felt light-headed. When she closed the bathroom mirror, her reflection startled her.

Her hair was the color of coffee with cream and normally flat with hardly any curl. After wearing the goggles and dealing with hoods and running for a day, her ponytail hung loose and frizzy. Her clothes had seen much better days, especially her ripped pants.

Clint stood in the open doorway and stifled a yawn. The poor man had been awake for three days. "Trouble sleeping?"

She swallowed hard and stared at him, unable to stop. "Yeah. My leg is bothering me." Along with everything else. She reached for the bottle of pain reliever she'd found in the med kit and took two.

"Looks like you got it taken care of." He nodded once toward the wrap.

She tried to smooth her hair around her face. When she hadn't known how messy she looked, her hair hadn't bothered her. Now that she'd seen the chaos springing up around her face, she wanted to shower and tame it.

The sleepiness that threaded his voice a moment before disappeared now. "You look fine. You have nothing to worry about."

He was all wrong. She had to keep that in the forefront of her mind. He was good at protecting her, but she had to protect her heart. Every man before him had run at the first sign of intelligent life or had felt threatened by her brain. She didn't want to believe he'd be just like them, but she hadn't wanted to believe it then either.

"I'll take my turn to watch." She waited for him to move.

He didn't seem all that willing as he stood in the doorway. "Do we need to talk? I feel like we probably should…"

She shook her head much more vehemently than his statement warranted. Talking was the last thing she wanted to do outside of her own complicated thoughts. This had to stay business. She may want to kiss him again if they delved into what a relationship might mean. But wanting something, and doing it even though it was wrong, weren't scientifically compatible.

"I don't think that's a good idea. We're both still tired and would probably regret talking right now." Was that what she had? Regrets? Her first and possibly only kiss couldn't be one she looked back on with disappointment.

"I can't make you talk but I'm just putting it out there that I think we should." He stepped to the side to let her by.

She slipped past him and found his seat by the window where he'd been watching and settled in to take her turn. With Clint a room away, she still felt safer than anywhere else in Yellowstone, even with the prickly feelings bubbling between them. Clint would never force her into talking if she didn't want to.

She'd taken their relationship down a path with no U-turns. A path that might lead her out of Yellowstone, for good.

* * *

All Clint's life, he'd prided himself on maintaining control. With Tamala, it was like juggling fire. He never knew what to expect or where his feelings would pop up next. He hadn't expected her to push back at him so resolutely.

How to do what he'd promised without thinking about her as the woman who'd rapidly captivated his heart? Denying himself would be impossible. That kiss had thrown him over the edge. He'd gone from wanting her in his life after this mess to needing her in his life right now.

All because he hadn't backed away.

He should've pulled back. He should've known a kiss right after they'd run from a killer would be nothing but an attempt to ease the stress. He'd been available. If he hadn't been there, she'd have used some other mechanism.

Obviously, from her stance afterward, the emotions meant nothing to her. Part of him wished he could be so flippant about what they'd done. The other was very glad he couldn't. A kiss should mean something. He'd never shared a "just because" moment with a woman before. If lips were involved, his heart was.

But now what? Make her talk about the kiss? Did he really want proof of his suspicions? That would only serve to make him angry, a feeling he hated. He strode to the kitchen and stuck his head in the fridge.

Nothing looked interesting or appetizing, despite his hunger, but he had to eat and he had to calm down his temper, so the refrigerator served two purposes. After settling on the rest of the chicken Tamala had put back, he sat down at the small table in his office.

From that vantage point he saw her sitting at the window. He said a prayer that she wouldn't see anything out there. He doubted he'd be able to sleep any better, worrying about the poachers and leaving her to watch.

He moved to the sofa, but left the door open. Everything they'd said, and didn't say, kept him awake and guessing. After a few hours of tossing and turning, he gave up and went to the window.

Mark's truck would never get out of his parking spot without a few hours of shoveling, and unless there was a good melt, the truck was stuck until April. From now— early or not—until the snow accumulated enough for oversnow vehicles, they were trapped.

He shook the feeling of dread from his spine. The fog was slightly easier to see through than the snow and he made out distant security lights, but everything else was dark. They'd shut the Old Faithful Inn down for the season, leaving it completely empty. He saw the tall, peaked roof in the distance, covered in a blanket of bright white.

When they neared the end of winter season, some of the Yellowstone team would take a day to carefully clear all the heavy snow off the roof. The weight was unimaginable. Nothing else moved that he saw, but somewhere in the park a poacher had to be planning what to do next.

If her attacker didn't sleep, he couldn't either. They needed a plan. He hated being one step behind on everything. A text came through on his phone and he went over to where it charged on the wall.

I looked at the Hummer. Had nothing else to do with all this snow. It was wiped pretty clean. I got no prints from it. There was a partial on one map, but it wasn't in the database when I sent it off to Cody. Though the stuff in the back seat is suspicious, you and I both know we can't arrest anyone based on that. The truck was a rental, but whoever rented it used an assumed name. We called the rental company to come get it when they plow the roads. Will keep if you think we need to.

The Hummer had led to nothing. That clue, like the tent, was another dead end. The maps hadn't told him any information, other than what he'd already known; they knew where Tamala worked and lived.

Her secrecy about his potential involvement had bothered him at first, but he could see now why she had. She'd been doing her job, tracking bears in their habitat, for years and had never found any evidence to contradict the theory that someone at the top was involved.

Until he'd needed her to trust him and she'd only trusted the rest of the Yellowstone rangers because of him. Which was why he fundamentally hated secrets. They tore at the very fabric of understanding. Even if she found he was right, she might hold a grudge against his team because he'd pushed her trust. It wasn't earned.

Tamala captured his mind, his heart and his eye. Her mistrust or not made him want to see the world differently, more forgiving. She was a triple threat, and he was helpless against the growing attraction between them.

TWELVE

Coffee, steaming and fragrant, filled Tamala's cup. She wrapped her hands around the mug like a lifeline. A day and a half with no sign of the poachers, and she almost felt refreshed.

Maybe she'd been right. They'd left. The race through the blizzard had been too much for them. They wouldn't be able to cope with the cold. Maybe they didn't want to miss their opportunity to get out of the park unseen. They'd lost interest. She had to believe that.

Clint sat down and topped off his own mug. "The snow is too deep to do any more moving around until we can recover our skis or until we mark the safe areas. It's not a good idea to go wandering around Yellowstone without knowing what you might walk into."

She knew the warnings but appreciated that he was as uncomfortable as her and needed talk to fill the overly quiet room. She was the one who warned visitors to stay on the paths. Some sites weren't open for close viewing during the winter months because of accessibility.

Without the case to distract her from Clint, she wasn't sure what to do besides pretending to drink her coffee.

Her leg was fine, if sore. Thank the Lord her shooter had been trying to ski and aim at the same time, or she'd be in a much worse state. "If we can't investigate, what do we do with today? Will they plow the road?"

He nodded briefly. "If the snow is deep enough, they'll groom the road every day for oversnow vehicles during the winter season. If there's not, they'll plow for administrative vehicles before switching over to oversnow travel."

"Except we have no way to travel over snow," she pointed out. Now she understood why the attacker kept on them when they'd tried to leave Yellowstone, and why the back of her mind said the poacher had to be within Yellowstone administration. They had to know all the rules that she didn't even know. With the deep snow and travel restricted to oversnow vehicles, she and Clint were sitting ducks. "Do you keep a snowmobile here, in Yellowstone?"

He nodded absently. "I do. It's in storage. But the trek to it won't be easy. We also can't use it until the roads are groomed, so it makes no sense to consider. No riding off the trails or you risk death, as you know."

She rubbed her temples and flinched. She'd risked death enough. This was Yellowstone, where snow into June was common. They were experts at snow management.

"Is it possible to dig Mark's truck out? Can I go out in the daylight to help?" She shivered, glancing at the bright sun out the window. Now that the fog had burned off, the temperature would be cold without cloud cover to hold in the heat.

"I don't think there's any need. As long as we're here,

we're safe. He hasn't found us yet. My only worry is that my office has little food. I'll have to go back to my place soon and bring some. I think, after that car left, that we're down to just one man."

"One?" She closed her eyes and tried to recall all they'd been through. There had been at least three in her cabin, but was it possible only one remained?

"I think so. They were a pack when they ransacked your home. Since then, we've only seen one. I think they chose one to leave behind—probably the one who rented the Hummer and ran us off the road—and the others left in a vehicle no one knew they had here. Maybe they took Meghan, thinking you'd said something to her. I believe they planned to stay as long as they could hide. I can't figure out what their endgame is. Getting out of here won't be easy. Maybe they'll use Meghan, since she has access as an employee."

She hadn't considered that and shivered, praying Meghan wasn't with them, that she'd just found a ride with someone and left the park early. The odds had seemed so out of proportion, she'd assumed there were still more than one of them. Though, neither of them could know for sure.

"Do you think that parking pass was hers? And how do you think he follows our every move?"

Clint took a deep breath, his solid chest rising and falling. "I think he's hiding out nearby. Maybe moving daily so no one gets suspicious. I'm going to watch for his tracks. If I see marks where there weren't any before, that might be our guy. I don't think the pass was hers."

After a slow sip of her cool coffee, she agreed. Sitting

there talking out the whole situation with him—like remaining sheltered with him—was just the way life should be.

The familiarity made her think about the kiss and all the reasons Clint was good for her, instead of the bad. She'd always known she couldn't settle for any handsome guy. He had to be intelligent. He had to love the outdoors and respect all God's creations. He had to see her as a partner in every way. Clint was that guy.

Yet something stood in their way. His past, for one. There was a lot she didn't know about him. He had to have a reason he was still single, and that reason was probably why he didn't trust easily or keep trying to reach out like she wanted to.

"What's one regret you have?"

"About the case?" He cocked his head. "I missed something."

She laughed, not wanting to talk about the chain of thoughts she'd had leading her to ask the question. "Not the case, just life. I don't really know you. I was thinking about a few of my own, so I wanted to know if I was alone."

He shifted in his seat, looking more uncomfortable than when she'd pushed him away. "I don't have many. The few I do have I don't talk about."

She'd hoped since she'd trusted him with the few details that meant life or death, he could trust her. They had nothing better to do than talk if they weren't going out to find the tent or the skis. "So maybe I'm one of them?" Voicing her concern didn't make the topic any easier.

"I don't think of things that happened in the last week as regrets. I can change those things. You can't go back and fix the past." He stood and dumped the few drops of coffee from his cup into the sink. "If you really want to know, my biggest one was letting myself be vulnerable and trusting that everyone who cared was honest. Sometimes, people keep things from you."

Tamala poured another cup of coffee to settle the aching in her chest. No wonder Clint was so big on trust. His had been broken.

He never talked about Mary with anyone. Ever... She'd been his wife for such a short time, but he'd loved her. The plan had been for her to visit her parents during the winter season because she missed them.

Mary hadn't told him she wasn't feeling well. He'd told himself for years that she hadn't known at the time. But winter break was so short. She'd said she would never keep anything from him. Maybe she'd felt like she was saving him, but keeping her secret gutted him. Stole his chance to see her. To tell her he loved her. To say goodbye.

He'd gotten a call from her parents about a week before the end of the season that she was in hospice and he should come quickly. By the time he'd found someone who could do his job for a week while he was gone, he'd ended up standing beside her casket, not her bedside.

His heart had been hollow for so long after that. Now he required honesty from everyone. Especially himself. If Mary knew... He shook the thought away. It was possible she hadn't known, wasn't it? Why else would she have left him and not said a word?

Every time someone lied or kept things from him, the pain of Mary's silence came crashing back in on him.

Regret didn't begin to cover it. The wound seemed to get worse over time, not better. The longer he went without talking, the less he wanted to bring her up.

Tamala went on, "Vulnerability isn't always bad. It is in this situation, and obviously in the one you're talking about, but it isn't inherently bad." She reached for his hand for a moment, then pulled back.

"Maybe. But when you open yourself up and think your entire future is planned, only to find out things weren't what they seemed, that kind of vulnerability will teach you a lesson." He would not talk about Mary. From the moment he'd heard of her illness, he'd known what he'd always suspected was true. He'd loved her deeply, but she'd cared little for him. Tamala would probably become another piece of his past in time. He couldn't trust himself, or his feelings again, even if he expected complete honesty—a relationship would fail.

"I might not know her name, but I think I know her face. She's the woman in the picture back in your room, isn't she?" Tam's eyes softened and she sighed. "I never had one person who hurt me so badly to cause disappointments. I had an entire class of them instead." She shuddered and ducked her head.

She'd turned the subject back to herself and he didn't want the spotlight back on him. "An entire class?" He wasn't sure how she'd known Mary was the woman in the picture, but she was right.

"My classmates thought my intelligence was funny. They thought reading was boring. The older I got, the more they teased I'd never have a boyfriend because guys don't like smart girls."

She shrugged, her eyes turning glassy for a moment

before she blinked the tears away. "I guess they were right. I've been single my whole life, so that qualifies under your definition of regret. I can't change my past and it's been longer than a few weeks."

He held in a flinch. He'd known intelligent people to compete because intelligence was limited to subjects. He could be an expert on bison but appear uneducated when it came to bears. And he didn't want to look uneducated to the present company.

"I don't want to be condescending so I won't say anything other than I can't believe people would be that shortsighted."

Of all the reasons to avoid a relationship with this woman, her brain was not one of them. He found her intelligence extremely attractive, especially when he already knew she had a heart of gold.

"I appreciate that. There's nothing I can do to change what they said now and I don't plan to go to any reunions, especially when my single status proves them right."

To keep himself from reaching out to her, he shoved his hands under the table. "Doesn't sound like you're missing much. Just because you went to school with people doesn't mean they are well suited to you."

She nodded slowly. "Most of them were hostile to any type of faith, so that played a part, too. Now I'm careful to pick friends who are at least accepting."

When he hired crews to work at the park, he told them about churches in the area and tried to mention offhandedly which ones he'd been to. Since he told them about other amenities, those who didn't care never seemed to mind, but those who did were thankful for the information. Churches weren't easy to reach in Yellowstone.

He took a deep breath and let his feelings about Mary bubble to the surface. In the past, thinking about her clouded every aspect of his life. He'd spent years mourning. Now she seemed in the distant past. Knowing about Tamala and what made her dig deeper into her studies and avoid men helped him see her more clearly.

Maybe she wanted the same from him. She might even need him to be vulnerable. Without the anguish, he might be able to talk about his needs. Which meant he could heal. "Her name was Mary. She was so smart and active here in the park. She got along with most and even loved those she didn't get along with. I fell pretty hard and we had what I thought was a great life for all of one year." He scrubbed a hand down his face, hating the scruff that had grown over the past few days. "She left to visit her parents over the winter season and died of a highly aggressive bone cancer a few weeks later."

"You let her in your heart, and she never said goodbye," Tamala offered.

"That's part of it. More so, I gave her all I had and felt guilty about my doubts in her love for me. She never told me she was sick. I wish I'd known… Her parents told me they'd called me because they thought I should be there, not because she wanted me there. She didn't ask for me. Some things you can get over. Some become permanent."

Tam laid a hand over his, not hesitating this time. "I have always had trouble forgiving those people who tormented me. After I realized I'd buried my head in my studies and avoided relationships of all kinds, I couldn't forgive them. I messed everything up so I couldn't be wrong—because you can't be ignored if you're the one avoiding people—and by doing so, they were right."

He hadn't considered forgiving Mary. What good would forgiveness do? It wasn't like she could help dying of cancer, and she could never apologize for falling out of love with him. Absolving her wouldn't bring her back, so he'd never considered it important. Now he understood. With Tamala's slight prodding, he'd given up his secret.

"I never thought about forgiving. I've been so focused on moving on I didn't see the value in looking back."

"I'll promise not to hide in my books anymore if you let yourself be vulnerable once in a while?" The corner of her mouth tipped slightly.

He was pretty sure he was keeping that promise this very moment. His heart sure raced like it exposed him for the universe to see. "What does *not* hiding in your books look like, exactly?"

She laughed, and a pretty blush crept up her cheeks. "I guess if anyone asks me to prom, I won't tell them I have a research paper due, so going wasn't possible."

No one did that. Did they? "You didn't really say that?"

She slowly shook her head. "No, but I imagined it. No one asked me. But I told myself I was busy, even if someone had asked. Making up a reason kept the sting away. A little." She shrugged and took her cup of coffee to the sink, then turned to face him. "I guess if I'm going to keep that promise, I'm going to have to survive long enough to live it. What do we do next?"

He didn't want to think for a moment about her mortality. He agreed to protect her to the bitter end, and she'd have the chance to turn someone down if she wanted to. Just not him.

His pulse raced as he slowly flexed his fingers, feeling the buzz of tension flow through him. He really wanted her to turn down everyone else except him. Did that mean he was falling for her? At the worst possible time of his life.

THIRTEEN

Tamala paced, feeling like a caged animal.

She needed to know who these men were. What was the poacher's name and how was he connected to Yellowstone? These were things she needed her computer and special hot spot to find. If Clint had a hot spot and it worked after the storm, she could do some digging into the poacher's identity. He had told his cronies she'd find him with a little internet searching. Searching was safe behind closed doors. She could even send her findings to Clint's associates in other sections. Then, even if he caught her, someone could still find him.

Clint sat over at the table, tapping his pen on a tablet, buried in thought. He'd asked her a few questions, which hadn't let her relax in hours. What if the poacher had taken over her cabin, gaining access to everything she knew about the bears he hunted?

If they were there, they would be close enough to see the Old Faithful area, but not close enough to be in the way. Then again, her place didn't have heat now and would be very uncomfortable. Not to mention year-round staff could see their footprints from her door.

"I wish we knew what they were doing and where they are. Or if there is only one or still many or if they're even still in the park. If we figure out who they are, we might understand why silencing me is so important. Then you'd be a step closer to apprehending them."

Clint seemed to read her thoughts. "Instead of them always being one step ahead of us."

She'd had the same feeling. They had to have set up a base somewhere they had a visual on most of the Yellowstone housing, or they had tracked her. She had very few items with her. Most of what she owned remained at her place. She had a few pieces of clothing, her thumb drive and her phone.

"I looked for a few minutes the night of the attack, when his face was fresh in my mind. I didn't find him then."

She shivered at the thought of that day. Bear hides brought in a lot of money, but conservationists feared the magnitude of the current slaughter might eventually put the dangerous animals on an endangered list.

"Talk to me about what you *did* find that day, before the poacher showed up." Clint tapped his paper again and watched her.

She appreciated that he didn't discount her feelings as nothing. "I stayed hidden and tried to find my target bear. My objective was to see where these popular bears go daily and mark their route to keep a human eye on them. The next day, after the attack, I looked on the dark web to see if anyone dangerous was talking about Mama 228. I wish I'd been successful."

A pervasive negative feeling settled over her. Staying cooped up and hiding had the same feeling as losing.

Clint stood and strode to his snow gear. "Maybe this will help." He unzipped the front and pulled the leather satchel from an inner pocket.

"We've been through that." They'd looked through the contents and found nothing unexpected. Not much to go on.

"It's what we have. A direct clue. Maybe something in here will jog your memory if you look at it again. There are mostly receipts and garbage. At least they *tried* not to litter." He rolled his eyes.

Clint sat back down at the table and Tamala joined him. His tense energy was contagious, and she hoped there would be something more than what they'd noticed before. He pulled out three receipts and a handful of candy bar wrappers, the filthy rag, park pass and gloves.

"They certainly don't eat well." He laid the trash aside and turned the bag upside down, but nothing else fell out.

Her mind whispered to her all those wrappers belonged to the poacher, but how would she know that? Was it her gut, or did she want them to be a solid clue? "Something about those wrappers is bothering my mind, and I need to figure out what. The reason might be important." She stood and paced again.

"I can't imagine any of them would've had time for a chocolate addiction." Clint picked up one wrapper. "Some people use these as an energy booster."

"Maybe it's the brand. I'm not sure." She closed her eyes and tried to remember what made her brain think along that one specific path. "It's not like I've been around him much. I track the bears I can, but there's only one of me."

"I've noticed," Clint said, but didn't look up.

Heat rushed to her chest. He wasn't supposed to say things like that. He was supposed to pull back from her and stay there so she didn't fall hard for him. Especially with how he still loved his wife.

"The day I saw him…" She strode away from Clint, trying to think. The farther she got from him, the less comfortable she felt, but the easier her brain worked.

"Was he stopping for a snack break?" Clint sounded skeptical.

It wasn't that he'd stopped, it was that *she* had. For the same type of wrapper on the ground. "I wonder if he's diabetic?"

"What? How did you come up with that?" Clint narrowed his eyes at her like she'd lost her mind.

"He snacks. A lot." She strode to the table and picked up one of the receipts. "Look here, third line down, syringes. And I picked up another wrapper just like these that day. He has to be diabetic. That means he can't be staying where it's too cold because his insulin would freeze. Many types of insulin have to be kept at seventy degrees or they are ineffective. He has to be hiding where there's food or a place to store some."

"Not if he's only eating candy bars." Clint held up the wrapper. "I don't want to think about what that's doing to his mind. If he's letting his blood sugar drop, then spike, it's probably affecting his mental state. But, at least he's nearby. That's how he's one step ahead. He can probably see my office right now. But we already knew that much. What we don't know is how he's managing enough heat to keep the insulin, and himself, from freezing."

Tamala shivered as she headed for the windows and peeked behind the blinds with as little movement as possible. "Do you think he's watching?"

"I do and it's only a matter of time before he comes here." Clint swiped the wrappers into the trash and stood.

Her stomach clenched from something other than hunger. Only a matter of time…

Clint stared at Tam's wounded leg. He hadn't protected her. "I think you should stay here. Lock the door. Rest. I'll be quick. He hasn't found us here and it's been almost two days. It's safer here."

Every time he'd tried to keep her from getting hurt, he'd failed. This time he'd get what he needed and get back to her. As soon as the park roads were plowed and opened, backup would arrive and they'd finish this.

"The cut isn't bad. I either want to go with you or I want both of us to stay here and bar the door. Nothing we've done so far has helped. Moving around has made him more bold and angrier."

He led her to the couch, and they both sat. The horizon loomed outside, a deep gray. More snow on the way.

"I'm frustrated, too. I usually do a lot more in the park, but I can't leave you alone to do my other work. But we need some supplies."

He didn't want to leave her alone as long as it would take him to check the housing around Old Faithful, but he didn't want to see her get hurt again.

"He found me here before." She hugged her legs to her chest.

"I don't want you to feel frightened." She should

feel safe and protected. "I put a wood dowel in the window so he can't get in there like he did at my place. The only other window that opens is this one, and I'll fix that, too. As long as you don't open the door, you should be fine."

"I don't like this. He's after me, but he shot at you, too. We should stay together."

He agreed in part, but he was trained, so he could get the supplies they needed. Could he watch over her and get what they needed? "I'm…worried."

She nodded her understanding. "So am I. But I don't think either of us will do any good by facing this alone. When the roads open, I want you to call in someone from Cody or Mammoth."

She finally trusted him enough to ask for help, but too late. If they were going to do that, they should've before the snow. There was no police force outside of Yellowstone that had the equipment to come through Sylvan Pass and take down an attempted murderer. The law enforcement rangers in Yellowstone were prepared, but a manhunt in the snow wasn't exactly common. Especially when the park was supposed to be all but shut down.

"I called the Mammoth team and they'll come when they can. Cody is out. We can't get through. Probably not safely for a long time. But we do have options. I have a few friends in the Jackson FBI office. If we need more help, that's where we'll find it. In the meantime, we need food. That's a priority." He wouldn't be able to use a snowmobile even if he had it with him until oversnow travel was approved, but if he had to choose, he'd rather stay with Tam.

"The FBI?" She turned away from him and raked her hair behind her ear. "Do you think they'd be able to take this on as quickly as we'd need them?"

He certainly would. This guy had hunted her and tried to kill both of them. He'd potentially crossed state lines since he had no idea where the man came from. Yellowstone was part of four states. That alone made an attempted murder case federal. He had no issue calling in a favor with his friends, assuming they could get through. The feds dealt with a chain of command, and sometimes requests took a long time to process, but this was urgent.

"I do. It certainly can't hurt to call and ask. If the request is urgent, as in life-threatening, they'll come."

He shoved another thick wooden dowel in the window. "There, a very cheap but effective lock."

"As long as he doesn't break the window or the doorknob or shoot it out. He's done that before."

He wanted to pull her into his arms and reassure her. She was stronger than this, but the fatigue of running from a killer weakened her resolve.

"Take me with you." She waited, holding his gaze.

"I don't want to put you in that danger. I…" He couldn't say what it would do to him if the poacher hurt her. Neither choice was a good one. Stay or go. Trust himself…or trust God to take care of them?

Clint led Tamala to the sofa and helped her sit, pulling the blanket around her and praying he was making the right decision. They had to have food but leaving her there, even for the few minutes it would take, left his throat dry and his blood pumping with worry.

With a wood-splintering crack, the door swung open and a huge man in a ski mask filled the doorway, a crowbar held above his head. Tamala screamed loudly and she shoved at him as the man pulled a gun from beneath his coat.

Clint locked his knees and reached for his own pistol. The poacher came at him fast. He aimed for the poacher and fired. The man was knocked back with a groan but managed to roll and quickly take aim at Tamala again.

She launched herself over the back of the thick sofa, but coils and padding wouldn't be enough to stop a bullet. Clint sprang to his feet and sprinted, aiming at the man's midsection.

The moment his shoulder hit the poacher, he understood why his bullet had been ineffective. How did the man have a bulletproof vest? The thick protective gear sent fissures of pain down Clint's body like he'd run into a brick wall.

"I've tried to kill you enough times. I'm finished with you," the poacher growled.

Clint raised his arm to ward off the blow, but the poacher hit him with the butt of his pistol and his world went black.

Tamala's breathing came too quickly as she tried to dislodge the gag the poacher had used to silence her. Fibers filled her mouth and she wiggled to get away. How could he take her prisoner in the middle of the day? There weren't many people left in Yellowstone, but someone was sure to see him. Someone would come to her rescue before she ended up in his den.

Her eyes filled with tears at the sight of Clint lying

on the floor of his office, blood pooling by his temple. Was he dead? Her heart beat too fast; she couldn't think straight. What would Clint want her to do?

The poacher took the blanket Clint had wrapped around her a moment before and bound her tightly inside, so tightly even moving was difficult. She focused on breathing. If she passed out, she couldn't call for help once he removed the mitten. If he ever did.

She couldn't see anything but felt him toss her over his shoulder, knocking the wind out of her. Tamala squeezed her eyes shut tight. *Lord, please let someone be out there to see him and stop this...* She tried to straighten or do anything that might make him have to slow down, to struggle, but nothing worked against the tight blanket around her.

Mark's flashlight in Clint's eyes woke him with a start.

"Where's Tamala?" He rubbed his head and regretted the movement instantly. "We've got to find her." He prayed she wasn't dead. How long had he been out?

"We've been looking. Everyone I've seen belongs in the park. With only a few employees left, there aren't many people to check."

Clint managed to push himself off the floor. His head pounded. "Let's look again. We'll find something." He donned his own bulletproof vest and coat, then headed outside.

There were snowshoe tracks around and a few of the maintenance staff worked outside the Old Faithful Inn. He waved to Mr. Henderson, one of the crewmen, on his way past Old Faithful and quickly warned him to watch for anyone, even people he knew, heading for the ranger office, and to let him know immediately if he saw anyone.

The visitor cabins sat off in the distance toward the huge Geyser Basin. Close enough that, if the poacher camped there and had binoculars, they probably monitored his house, maybe Tamala's, too, and definitely his office. He kept close attention to the ground. There shouldn't be any tracks near the visitor cabins. The locks had been secured even before the snow.

The crew was small enough that he knew where each one lived. All the homes with tracks were areas that should have them. He didn't see any out of place. A quick stop at the Snow Lodge was also a dead end. Looking through frost-covered windows, he discovered no one was there and the counters and tables were bare. If someone had hoped to seek food or shelter there, they would be disappointed. But so was he.

The team working near the resident housing waved at him to hurry and ran while he was still a few yards away. Apprehension ticked at the back of his neck. Even when buffalo or bear wandered too close, the workers didn't run. They knew the protocol.

He jogged after them until he realized they were heading toward his office. They might've heard Tamala. He took off, racing for his front door, overtaking the other crew.

"We heard someone screaming in the walkie. We thought it was Tamala and came as fast as possible." Mr. Henderson got there a moment after Clint.

His home walkie, the one he used when he wasn't on duty, sat on his desk. It crackled to life. "Are you out there, Clint? I didn't hit you that hard." A bitter laugh ricocheted through the room.

He moved to the device and pressed the talk button. "I'm here. Tell me where she is."

Mr. Henderson stood by his side as Mark took a visible deep breath.

"Tell you? That would be no fun. Come find us. But your time is running out." The silence filled the room until Mark spoke.

"I've checked around the inn, the clinic, all the places usually only open to tourists where we hadn't looked before."

The others nodded in thought. "No one can move fast in this snow, they have to be close."

On the table lay the little stuffed bear that used to hang from the zipper of Tamala's backpack. Clint hadn't noticed it before when he'd left to search. The poacher was toying with them now.

He faced the small group. "Tamala, one of our naturalists, is being hunted by a group of poachers. She saw one of them try to kill a bear here in the park." He wanted to give them extra reason to watch for the one man in particular. "One of them wants her dead. Both of us agree he seems familiar, so he may be someone from the park or connected financially. We know that he stands to lose a fortune if Tamala figures out who he is and reveals his identity." He pointed to the bear plushy. "He left a calling card. That belonged to her."

"So, how do we help? We didn't see anything." Mr. Henderson eyed the walkie, then Clint.

He refused to actively enlist the engineering team, and legally, he couldn't. Those men didn't sign on for that kind of danger and didn't work for him. "Have you seen anyone around who you recognize, but who shouldn't be here? Anyone you thought may be new this year?" His mind whirred for a moment. "Or maybe someone you did recognize, but thought was out of place?"

One man slowly nodded and elbowed Mr. Henderson.

"We saw someone like that yesterday. Didn't seem to know any of us, but insisted he worked for the park. He didn't take off his ski mask, but we were outside, so that wasn't completely strange. We gave him a job to do and let him be. I never went to check if he did it."

That would be the guy. There were no new people who'd joined the engineering team that season. "Any idea where he might be staying?" This was his only lead, and he was so tired he wasn't sure what questions to ask.

Mr. Henderson looked pensive. "When we saw him, he left toward the naturalist cabins. I only remember because the job I sent him to do was in the opposite direction. I've never seen someone new come in this time of year, but I didn't want to push the guy."

"It's best you didn't." They hadn't checked Tamala's since her home wasn't secured. That made it the most likely place for him to be, where he'd probably assumed they'd never check. "Anything else about him you remember?"

The men thought for a moment, but all shook their heads. Another dead end. Was it possible one of his team was the poacher? He hadn't wanted to believe it.

"I'll head that way. Call up Harley over at the Mammoth Hot Springs office for backup. They'll need to rush snow removal. Hopefully, I can get Tamala out of there and have this situation in hand by the time they arrive."

Mr. Henderson nodded. "I'll keep my walkie with me. That new guy did have a walkie, like someone who works in the park. I won't let her know you're on the way though, in case he's listening in."

Clint nodded. "Good idea. If she's listening, you can let her know you're here. It'll help her. But don't say anything about me."

Henderson handed him the key to his sled. "Take this, you'll need it."

Clint patted him on the shoulder as a thank-you. He knew using the machine was life-threatening before oversnow vehicles were approved, but desperate times called for desperate measures and he headed out into the storm.

FOURTEEN

Tamala closed her eyes, wishing her home felt safe like it should and focused on the sounds outside her bedroom door. If she had something to do with her mind, she wouldn't think about what might happen any moment. Her room was now her prison, and the poacher had strapped her to a chair. She waited for what he'd do next.

Something about him was familiar, but the memory wouldn't come. Her mind refused to work, like when she met someone she knew at a store and they weren't in the environment where she normally encountered them. A block had formed, preventing her from discerning where she knew him from. But she did know him and that made him even more dangerous.

He sat on the floor, carving lines into the old wood planks. "We'll give Clint another few minutes. Thought for sure he'd have come for you by now. Don't know why. You're not much of anything." He held up the machete. She shuddered at the blade that was at least twelve inches long.

"Once he gets here, I'll take care of two birds and I don't even need a stone. A bullet will do."

He laughed at his own joke. "Birds. You two have been together so much lately, maybe you're lovebirds?" He plunged the knife into her floor.

She wanted to shout but the gag prevented any sound. As far as she'd seen, he worked alone now. He'd spoken to no one else, and when he'd brought her in, no one had been there. Almost immediately, he'd locked her inside her room and hadn't left. She prayed Clint would be careful, but knew he'd come. He protected the people in his park, even the ones who hurt him.

"I left enough clues for him to find us. I'm ready to go home and warm up. This has taken far longer than it should and he's to blame for that."

So, he wanted Clint to pay for the wasted time, maybe more than he wanted her dead. She pulled against the binding tying her hands, trying to stretch the rope. The rough grains rubbed into her wrists. If she freed herself and made a run for it, the window was near enough for escape.

If she didn't take a chance, he'd kill her anyway. He'd already described in gruesome detail exactly how he'd do it. Clint was an annoyance to him. She'd turned into his fascination. Much like Mama would be a trophy he couldn't show anyone, so would she be. Part of her worried that once he'd killed, he'd enjoy it more than hunting bears and his killing wouldn't stop with her and Clint.

The loud crackle of the walkie sounded on the floor next to him. "Tamala? You there?" came a voice too garbled to recognize.

She froze as he held his finger to his mouth for quiet and picked it up. He held his long knife in one hand

and the walkie in the other, but he didn't press the talk button.

"If you say anything about where you are, you'll regret it." He touched the tip of the knife to her arm and a bead of blood formed instantly. "Understand?"

The frigid room had stolen most of her feeling. Fascinated by the fact that the cut didn't hurt yet, she didn't respond as she watched her blood pool. *Get it together, Tam!* She nodded as sweat prickled over her skin, finally making the nick burn. He removed the mitten from her mouth and she choked on the dryness. He pressed the button on the walkie and held it up to her mouth. "All clear. False alarm. You read?" Talking scratched her throat.

The line crackled and then went dead. To someone who never listened, it would sound like nothing, but she'd distinctly heard *Jackson*.

"What did he say?" He leaned over her and his blade hovered inches from her neck.

"He said, 'ten four.' It means he understands." She closed her eyes and tried to press back into the chair as far away from the knife as possible.

"Good. I want Clint here and no one else. This party is for him."

If she'd heard correctly, he'd get his wish. Clint *Jackson* was coming. If she managed an escape before he got there, they'd finally be one step ahead. They'd know where to find the poacher and Clint could help her remember who this man was. He'd helped jog her memory with the wrappers.

He drew back and stared at her, tracing her jaw with his finger. If she bent her neck any further, she'd strain her muscles. He gripped her chin to force her eyes on him.

"Mine will be the last face you see. Better pray while you have the chance." He turned and left.

Her chest rose and fell as hot tears pierced the sides of her eyes. *Lord, help!* She'd found herself calling out more and more the deeper she got into this mess, and now she needed a way out. By wiggling her hands she'd slipped the rope lower, but it caught on the widest part around her palms and now she was stuck.

There was a short, sharp knock on the window and when she twisted to see what made the sound, Clint crouched flat outside. He held up his finger to his lips for quiet as he slowly pried the window open.

After it slid a few inches, he reached in and shoved the sliding glass the rest of the way. The faint *creak* of the friction seemed loud to her ears, deprived of noise. He whispered softly, "Don't make a sound. I'll get you untied, then we run."

She hated running, but safety sounded too good. The killer was finally out of the room, and she hadn't seen his gun once. "Should we take him?"

Clint shook his head as he climbed through the window. "Not now."

The door burst open and the poacher stormed in, his ski mask still covering his face. "I'm so tired of your interference." He raised his gun.

Tamala screamed as Clint tipped her chair over, slamming her to the floor and out of the way. He jumped back, trying to find a defensive position as he went for his gun. "Run!"

She tugged on her arms, finding he'd loosened the rope enough to free her. Her head swam as she pushed to her feet.

There was no way she would leave Clint to face the killer alone, not after she'd insisted they stick together. Not now that she knew what the killer was capable of. He held out the gun, trying to cover both of them. She tugged Clint toward her. There was no doctor to mend up either of them if the killer got too close.

Clint leaped forward, pinning the poacher's wrists and holding him against the wall. If she did anything from her vantage point, she'd be more likely to hurt Clint.

With a quick spin, the poacher took the upper hand and shoved Clint against the wall. He towered at least six inches over Clint and was at least a hundred pounds heavier.

No matter how hopeless the situation seemed, she couldn't force her feet to run. The killer had to have another gun nearby. She raced to the kitchen and saw her assailant's coat draped over a chair. In the right-hand pocket she found it. She grabbed it and rushed back into her room.

"Let us go, or I'll shoot." After all he'd put her through, she wanted to shoot anyway. Her hand shook as she raised the pistol and took aim. Dread gave her tunnel vision. Was she sure of her aim, and could she deal with the consequences if she hit anyone?

He laughed from his position against the wall. With a huge grunt he punched Clint in the stomach. There was no way out of the tiny room besides the window. Clint doubled over, but his gaze caught hers. "Tam, run." While he looked weakened, the order was anything but.

She had to choose to either help Clint or keep her aim on the poacher. Let him go, or help the man she was growing to love.

Tamala cocked the pistol and fired wide. The poacher laughed hysterically as he made a quick shot, blasting out her bedroom window. She covered her head as she landed on her knees. Clint raised his weapon and fired as the killer dove through her missing window.

Clint stumbled to his feet and took after him at a run.

The words the poacher had said to her twisted her stomach. For her and Clint, this was life or death. For him, it was a game. Just another kill like the bears he hunted. Apprehension tickled the back of her neck. She hated to be alone now. As she headed out into her living room at a run, she found Clint outside, kneeling in the snow clutching his chest where he'd been punched.

"He got away, again." His frustration tore at her insides. If she'd managed to shoot properly…

He tried to stand, using the building for support.

"Wait. I haven't looked at that yet." She helped him to his feet. Her heart hitched, and she closed her eyes for a moment. When she was ready, she forced herself to look at the open stripe of red down his front.

"It doesn't look too deep."

"Good. Feels like he sliced me in half. He must have been holding something in his hand when he hit me." He laughed and tried to release the wall but wobbled.

"Let's get back to the office and clean you up."

He glanced at her window, winced and sucked in his breath as he held his side. "I'll send Mr. Henderson over to board this up." He slipped his arm around her shoulders and leaned against her. Grabbing the walkie from next to the wall where it had landed, he adjusted the frequency and pressed the talk button.

"Mark, I'm going to need your assistance down in

bungalow number five. Armed suspect on the loose. Need backup."

Tamala caught his eye and knew she had never trusted someone so much. This wasn't about having to, it was about believing in the man who would protect her.

His cut wasn't too bad, but gave him a good excuse to hold tight to Tamala and lean on her a little. Mark had checked the area and now walked a few paces ahead of them. He'd always thought seeing his own life flash before his eyes would be scary but seeing Tamala's had been terrifying. That machete would be branded in his memory for a long time. At least now they knew where he'd been hiding out. The betrayal that one of his own had turned still cut worse than the knife.

Cold air hit the gash on his stomach, and he remembered his coat was sliced up. He tugged the two edges closed and held tight. The chill against the heat of the wound made his head spin.

The second round of snow would add to what was already deep in areas. Bad roads would keep the FBI from getting there, especially within Yellowstone. They were covered in at least four feet of snow. That left him few resources outside the other park law enforcement rangers. Mark touched his hat. "I'll call the team and update them about what happened. I'll be right here to stand as a lookout." He ducked his head and quietly took cover near the corner of the ranger station.

"We've got to act fast. I told the engineering team to call Law Enforcement Ranger William Grainger." He wanted to show her he would be completely open with her about the case.

The realization hit him harder than the punch. He was falling for her. No question about it. If the poacher hurt her again, he refused to contain himself. No one would hurt her. Pinpointing when the change had happened was impossible, but it was as certain as the snow pelting them.

"I think we both need a long talk together when this isn't looming over our heads."

He pushed the door open to the inner office. She switched on the light and the bright bulbs of the overhead light seemed strangely cold. He didn't want to see the inside of his medical kit again for a long time.

Tamala led him over to the small table meant for questioning suspects and sat him on a chair against the wall. At least she wasn't going to ask him to bandage himself up.

She frowned as she tugged on his shirt to see the cut more clearly, then she opened up to him about what happened. "He told me more while I was a captive there. Things that may help you figure out who he is. He said he used to run this park and could do whatever he wanted. If they hadn't found out, he'd still be here, doing as he pleased." She closed her eyes, gripping the cleaning gauze above his wound. "I'm assuming he means the park service, concessioners don't act like they own the park." She held her breath as she dabbed the gauze against his wound.

"Used to, as in *removed*?" His mind whirred with ideas. Working for the park was an honor and the huge majority of people who were hired treated it like the privilege it was. He touched her arm. "They shot at you, and I can't protect you from that."

She shook her head as she nudged his shoulders to the wall and examined the damage closer. He shrugged out of his coat and shirt, finally looking at the injury. A diagonal slice across his abdomen marred his fading tan from summer.

"If we catch him before he can regroup, we'll have him. Plus, I have his gun. We can do this. All I have to do is walk outside and I'd be bait. We could end this." She patted the back of her waistband.

"You have *one* of his guns." The poacher had at least one other, maybe more if he was a former ranger and was fully trained as an officer, as Clint was beginning to suspect. "That weapon won't do us a bit of good until we're close enough to him to be in danger. He's escalating, and he's getting increasingly bold." He held out his hand for the pistol.

With slow precision, she took it from her waistband and handed him the firearm. He didn't want trust to matter so much to him, but it did. That and faith were the basis of any good relationship, and he needed those to move forward. No matter how much he cared for her. They would have nothing without those.

"I need you to trust me. We will get this guy. I will personally make sure the right people come and take care of him. We'll bring him to justice and then we'll move ahead." Hopefully together, if he convinced her to give him a chance.

She stared at his chin, not in his eyes. "I believe you. I just have a different idea of how we should finish this." She ripped off a piece of medical tape and gently pressed it over a gauze square at the top of his wound.

He gathered her hands to keep her from using the

bandage as an excuse to ignore his thoughts. "But can you trust me and my team to come up with something we can both live with?"

He felt her pull away from him mentally. She'd decided what she thought was the best course of action and waiting wasn't it. How could he trust her if she didn't want to share the load? He rejected the idea of making herself bait, but if he didn't listen and pay attention to what she wanted, he might miss his chance to protect her.

"I think we'd be wise to wait."

She nodded slightly but still didn't look him in the eye. "Wise. I guess that's what I've always been. We'll talk more about what that means later." She handed him his shirt and turned away.

Tamala had turned as cold as the blizzard outside. She wanted to get the situation finished and he understood, but without the proper help, they might both wind up on the wrong end of a blade big enough to take out a bear.

FIFTEEN

Mark knocked on the office door to wake her the following morning and let her know Dave would be taking over protecting the outside. She hoped the additional help meant Clint had finally been able to rest, but she doubted it. If they could be done hiding, they could get back to life.

"Have you heard from Grainger yet?" She refused to look at Clint as she sat down in front of his desk. Grainger wouldn't be there until the next day at least. If he made it through the snow at all, but she had to fill the silence.

"Nothing, but the snow's coming down pretty hard."

She glanced at the boarded-up window, glad for the protection and the privacy. "I'm sure our poacher has left my cabin since it's now not only destroyed but open, so where would he go next?"

"My place…or maybe somewhere else."

"Should we go look? Before Mark leaves, maybe even take Dave?" She couldn't count herself as part of the manpower, but surely the three could take him down.

Clint pursed his lips. "I have a few things to do here

that I've put off. They can't wait. When I finish, we'll snowshoe over there."

She nodded her acceptance. At least he was listening to her idea. Clint had helped her this far because he'd felt he had to as the head law enforcement ranger in the Old Faithful area. She still wanted to finish the job and then go heal from her wounds at home, away from her need to be with Clint.

Smoke poured in from under the door and dread lodged in Tamala's throat before she tugged her shirt over her mouth.

"Tam?" Clint called for her but just as quickly she couldn't see him, the tiny room filled so quickly.

"Clint! I'm here. What's going on?" The smoke made her head hurt and she went for the door.

Behind her, Clint coughed. She heard him feeling his way around his desk. The smoke made her light-headed. She heard the *crack* of a pistol in the distance, just before the smoke stole her breath away.

SIXTEEN

Clint's head throbbed where he lay tied with his hands behind his back on the floor in a room he didn't recognize. He concentrated on getting past the pain and his vision came into focus. The poacher stood over Tamala, finally without a covering on his face. She bled from slight cuts all over, and a rush of adrenaline and anger urged him to act. He bent back, sliding his hands into his back pocket and retrieving the small knife there.

With a slight fumble, he flipped it open, trying to keep as still as possible. He now recognized the poacher, former Yellowstone Ranger Anders Boyce. He'd retired three years before. But now Clint wondered if his retirement had been encouraged by the park service.

He wouldn't notice Clint's movement if he stayed as still as possible. He took in his surroundings while he worked on the rope. There was little in the room. A few feet away, on a low shelf, sat an old can of bear spray. Better weapon than the small knife as long as it still worked. The rest of the room was fairly barren.

In a minute, he had his hands free. He'd have one shot. The moment he moved, Anders would be on him.

He tensed his muscles, forcing them to do what they didn't want to after lying on the floor so long. He leapt to his feet, grabbing the spray and flipping the top.

As Anders raced toward him, Clint blasted him full in the face with the spray. He didn't have time to be satisfied as Anders fell to his knees, screaming and covering his eyes, he had to free Tam and get them out of there.

Clint blinked back the burn from the spray as he grabbed the knife off the floor and cut Tamala free from the chair. Anders crawled on the floor, his face red and puffy, his eyes swollen. Streams of tears trickled down his cheeks. But the effect wouldn't last long. If the weapon wasn't gone...

Clint only had about fifteen minutes before the bear spray wore off to get Tamala somewhere safe. Now there would be no stopping him. Unless... He glanced at the zip tie that had been around Tam's wrist and flinched as he removed the tape from her mouth.

Get her to safety. The thought gave him the power to go on. "Where did he get those?" He hoped Tam could answer him and he wished for more time to take care, but moments raced by.

She groaned and closed her eyes in consternation. "From his sleeve. I don't know where he keeps them." She sounded so weak, and tears ran down her face, mixing with the cuts. Her hair lay tangled over her shoulder, like he'd yanked it. "Please, Clint. Get me out of here." Her head lolled back.

The poacher screamed with the burning in his eyes, but seconds counted. Tam had faced the same choice. Take out their attacker or rescue Clint. She'd chosen him. They'd get this guy when backup arrived, especially because he'd run out of places to hide. If Clint had run out, so had Anders. He helped her up as Anders stilled, squinting at them a few feet away. He had no rope, no cuffs with him and Anders had to have taken his gun. Without those zip ties, he had nothing to use to tie up Anders.

With slow deliberation, Anders squinted through his tears, trying to find them. The poacher slowly ran his arm over his eyes meeting Clint's gaze despite the tears, then slowly reached for his coat pocket and drew Clint's service pistol. He slowly swiveled his arm, looking, listening, both arms out.

Tamala sucked in a huge breath and yelled, "Clint! Run!"

Clint gripped her around the waist and flung them both outside into the snow as bullets flew through the air. A moment later, with all six rounds spent, all sound ceased. They only waited seconds before Clint shuffled Tamala into a nearby sled, gathered the pull string, and took off at a run.

Pinpricks of pain covered her from her face to her legs, but they weren't half as painful as the knowledge that this wasn't over. They'd had to leave Anders there. At least she'd been able to help, and they'd avoided Anders's unseeing, furious aim.

But if Clint hadn't managed to escape his ropes, she couldn't have survived the night. She was too weak to walk after their narrow escape.

When Clint veered the sled off toward the Old Faithful Inn, apprehension struggled against the knowledge that Clint wouldn't do anything to hurt her. Her brain was stuck in a fight or flight mindset, and she warred for control. He knew what he was doing. He wanted nothing more than to protect her, and Anders had taken that from him. The cold steel in his eyes when he'd torn the tape from her mouth still gave her a chill.

Her eyes burned and watered from whatever the smoke was and from the bear spray and Clint's probably did, too, but at least they were alive.

Clint helped her off the sled with the cold precision of a professional who'd seen all the evil in the world. Her knees wobbled and though she didn't want to, she clung to him to stay upright. There would be no heat inside the big old building. "Clint, why are we here?"

Snow hung in sheets off the slanted roof. It was beautiful, like a hanging carved scroll from the eave, even in the dark as more snow pummeled them. He avoided answering as he linked his arm tightly around her and led her to the door. While he hunted for the right key on his large key ring, her knees trembled under her weight. She struggled to stay upright. His help and strength were blessings.

Once the door swung open, he led her over to a big leather chair in the center of the lounge and sat her down. He turned and went into a back room she'd never realized was there. A minute later he returned with a big white bucket and a tall heater similar to the space heaters she'd seen used on patios.

"Will that work?" her voice quivered.

She hoped the mess the poacher had made of her didn't ruin the blanket, but she was damp and cold from the ride. Too cold to give up the cover now that she had it. Anders had taken her coat from her and torn it to shreds.

"It's kerosene. Should be fine in here since there's so much open air. We don't use them unless we have to. He'll never look for you here because I'm not supposed to have a key and he knows that fact. No one in the park should have a key. The concessioners gave it to me during an emergency last summer and didn't take it back. I'm going to go move the sled out far away from here. The wind and snow will take care of any tracks we left. I don't have much time. Stay put here and warm up. I'll return as soon as I can."

Without Clint at her side, it was her against Anders and she already knew how that would end. No one else completely understood her situation. He would find her, capture her and kill her. She was still surprised he hadn't when he'd had her.

"Don't go. The only time I feel like I'm going to survive is when you're here."

The time she'd spent with Anders, trying not to let herself slip into incapacitating fear, had been eye-opening. When she'd first woken up after he'd abducted them from Clint's office, Anders had claimed that, just like he'd planned to hunt Mama 228, and pin the poaching on Clint, he was going to kill her, pin the murder on Clint and get his job back. She'd been too terrified to argue with his flawed logic and worried that if she did, he'd simply kill her anyway.

Behind the front desk, there was a small first aid kit, and Tamala clutched the blanket tightly as Clint went to retrieve it.

"I will help you clean up, but I have to go see what

happened to Mark and Dave and you're too weak to come with me. I will barricade you in, but I can't leave them and I have no way of contacting them."

She wanted to nod, but her teeth chattered instead. Removing the blanket so Clint could tend to her made her tremble with shivers. Nighttime during the winter in Yellowstone was no time to be without heat.

There were antiseptic wipes and bandages in the kit, and Clint cleaned her off as much as possible without taking off anything. Her doctor would never believe her story when she went to see him after this was all done. Assuming she lived that long.

She would hold him back because of her injuries and, if he hurried, he was leaving her at the safest time while Anders was still blinded by the bear spray. Time was ticking though. "Okay, I understand. But hurry."

Tromping through thick snow used enough energy and concentration to keep Clint focused on something other than his frustration. Tamala had been right from the start about Anders. She hadn't known his name, but she'd known he'd worked for the park. Clint had worked under Anders when he'd started.

He needed a few minutes to himself to think about all the feelings roiling around inside of him. Frustration, hurt and fear over losing her. Then there was the fear of what he'd find back at the ranger station. What had Anders done to his men? Snow hit him in the face and chilled his neck. Zipping up his suit as far as it would go, he hunched into the wind. He didn't have time to ruminate, his team needed him and Tam needed him to return fast.

No one else moved around in the blizzard, meaning Ranger Grainger—what they called the Mammoth Hot Springs Head Ranger for fun—probably had prudently decided to wait to make the trip to the Old Faithful area until tomorrow. Getting stuck miles from the nearest tow truck in a blizzard was dangerous. He didn't blame Grainger for waiting, but when he arrived, they had to take care of Anders somehow.

Clint checked his watch and leaned into the wind, broadening his stride. By now, if Anders was one of the few who healed fast from bear spray, he'd be back to almost normal. Definitely able to walk around and be out on the hunt. Clint had a small flashlight he'd taken from the inn with him in case he needed it, but a beam of light would draw attention to himself. Knowing the hunter roamed free made him keep the light in his pocket. Tonight, attracting attention was the last thing he wanted to do.

Aside from Tamala, there was only one thing he wanted. He wanted that man arrested and out of his life for good. Then he wanted to send Tamala home to her family for the rest of the winter season to heal.

He couldn't sit by and watch her work when she returned like nothing had changed between them when they'd shared so much. He didn't want to let life pass him by anymore.

Once Grainger arrived, he outranked Clint and would take over the team. That would relieve some of the load on his shoulders. After he finished this case, he'd deal with his heart.

He kept on alert, looking for any movement. He saw lights on inside the ranger station and cautiously went inside. Without his weapon, he felt like a sitting duck. In the distance, he heard Dave talking on the phone and he breathed a sigh of relief as he headed for Dave's office.

He peered inside. Dave sat at his desk and when Dave glanced up he almost dropped his phone.

"Sir!" He pressed the phone back to his ear. "I'll call you right back. Clint's been found." Turning to Clint, he said, "Where did he take you?"

Clint held up his hand. "I don't have time right now. Where's Mark?"

"I called him back in as soon as I woke up. He hit me with a tranquilizer dart." Dave pointed to the evidence on the desk. "I'm so glad I didn't freeze to death out there."

"I need to get back to Tamala. Is Mark out looking for our guy?"

"Yes, sir."

"Radio him and tell him he's on the lookout for Anders Boyce."

Dave's mouth dropped open slightly. "Yes, sir."

He grabbed his spare pistol from his locked desk and rushed back to the Old Faithful Inn. When he pushed open the door, Tamala almost jumped out of her skin. She leaped to her feet, eyes bright and wide.

"You scared me."

"That's why I warned you I was coming back. Anything happen?" From this point forward, nothing mattered but arresting Anders. Their relationship had to have some barrier or he might let the distraction make him do something he would forever regret. He'd concern himself with her health and safety. Nothing more. At least for now. She'd cleaned up her face and hands even more than he had but looked so tired. If he stayed nearby, maybe she could get the rest she needed.

"No. Not a sound. I listened." She tucked herself back into the chair. "What will you do?"

He unzipped his snowsuit and hung it to dry over a chair, sat down on the other side of the heater, keeping space between them. Space he didn't want, but needed all the same.

"I'll stay here and let you sleep tonight, then I'll meet with some of my crew tomorrow so we can form a plan. This snow will hold them back, but Grainger has the resources to get here tomorrow."

She slowly nodded and scratched at her neck, then flinched. "I keep forgetting." Her eyes turned glassy as she stared at her fingers. "This is going to take a long time to heal."

He nodded, agreeing with her assessment and wondering if she meant more than her physical wounds. The damage would take time to heal on his end, too. Now that they knew the poacher had been on the inside, at least at one point. He wondered if she would trust Grainger. "What will you tell Grainger?"

She closed her eyes. "I saw Anders shoot at a bear in the park, that is fact. I know he ran us off the road and threatened to kill both of us multiple times. He's been stalking me ever since. I'll tell them his goal is to get his job back so he can poach whatever he wants, since he'll have access to the park. I'll tell him my friend Meghan is missing and no one has been able to reach her. I don't think he'll have to ask me, but I'll agree to testify against him."

He couldn't keep a slight smile of pride from his lips.

She sounded like she trusted his team, even knowing Anders had once been the leader. Maybe for his sake, but he couldn't let that puff his chest too much until this was over.

A tear ran down her face and she winced, swiping it away. He fought the urge to go to her, knowing she wouldn't want that right now. She'd kissed him by accident. She hadn't meant it.

"I'm going to sleep."

He wanted to argue, to try to get her to keep talking to him, but that would only make him want to be with her more. His heart's only protection would be just as destroyed as Tamala's bungalow. He turned his chair away from her to face the door. A night vigil was just what he needed to remind him of his purpose in all this. Protection, not affection.

SEVENTEEN

Every muscle in Tamala's back and neck tensed as she unfolded from the big leather chair in the lobby of the Old Faithful Inn. Her breath gathered in the air, and she realized the heater had run out of fuel while she'd slept. Frost covered the top of the blanket where her warm exhalation caught in the fibers.

The wood walls loomed dark and foreboding around her. Though the snow had stopped, and the sun had come up, a thick layer of clouds obscured the glow, illuminating sharp frost feather patterns on all the windows. The usually welcoming inn seemed more like a bleak cavern without people, light, heat, and sound.

She'd made it through the night alive and unharmed, though her skin burned and tingled with the cuts from her attacker's abuse the evening before. They needed treatment and cleaning, but there would be no hot shower soon. Today was the day Clint and his team would catch Anders Boyce.

Taking him on alone would be a mistake. She wasn't afraid of admitting her faults and miscalculations. This would be no easy takedown, and Anders would attempt to kill Clint or her on sight. Clint was the sole reason she was still alive, that and Anders's desperate need to toy with her like a captured mouse.

Law Enforcement Ranger William Grainger would finally arrive to team up with Clint and arrest the poacher turned attempted murderer. She'd written up a report last night with Clint's guidance detailing how the man had physically assaulted her. No holding back information. All worry about the involvement of her fellow Yellowstone workers, gone. Anders had chased and attacked her. Her body carried all the evidence needed. If Grainger got stuck on motive, she could tell him in all truth it was greed, multiple kinds of greed. Once they caught him, he wouldn't be able to hold back from detailing his plan. He'd been proud of it.

The thought stalled her in place. Did she really want to go back and follow bears in the spring after all this? Her work would never be the same again, knowing a situation like this could happen. The lonely Yellowstone trails seemed more frightening now that she'd been up close to the people who hid around them. Especially since Anders had, at one time, worked in the park.

She tugged the blanket tighter around her shoulders as she hunted for something to warm her a little. Clint hadn't told her what to do if the heater shut off, and he'd left early that morning, leaving Mark outside the front door to protect her. She didn't want to damage anything. Staying at the Old Faithful Inn with no food or heat wasn't really a cozy or long-term solution. There was more to life than safety, and Clint wasn't going to come back and take care of everything for her. And why would he when she'd shoved him away? Moving on was better for him if he didn't.

When she saw him next, she would break off whatever it was they had. No more kisses or pretending they weren't both thinking about each other. No more working as a team to catch her attacker.

She couldn't help but wonder if they would still feel anything on the other side of the stress of being hunted? Would they be able to have a normal relationship? He had listened to her first, then hadn't when she'd wanted to lure Anders. But he'd been right. She knew that now. But had her suggestion stopped him from trusting her?

Neither of them had trusted like they should. Admitting they'd doomed their relationship before it started was like closing herself in a prison.

She'd been sure with her biological studies and travel to various national parks she'd be alone forever. Her science and studies were her mates. Who'd want to marry a scientist, except maybe another scientist? All those she'd met were as disinterested as she'd been in long-term relationships. She certainly hadn't planned on falling for a rugged law enforcement ranger.

A key slid loudly into the lock, and she turned to the sound. Her attacker wouldn't have a key, nor would he let anyone know she was hiding there. The sound had to be someone in maintenance or Clint coming for her. Probably Clint, since she'd accused him of scaring her the night before. He still did things, like making sure she heard the key in the lock, so she'd be more comfortable. She wanted to see him one last time but also didn't because that signaled the end.

Clint stood in the doorway, his profile strong and inviting. "I have a coat for you. A plow made it through this morning, and Grainger followed. He's in my office waiting for your statement." He lingered close to the door, keeping distance between them.

She reached for the coat he offered and shrugged it over her shoulders. "Thank you."

She rolled the soiled blanket up and held tight to it. "I'll need to wash this anyway." She held up the corner of the wool blanket. "I'll follow you back to your office so they won't be waiting long."

He nodded and his firm mouth stuck in a harsh line, but his eyes held warmth she couldn't explain. Was he as ready to let go as she was? That would make the break easier on both of them.

"It should all be over soon."

Tears burned her eyes at his statement. "Clint...I'm sorry. I reached out to you when I was terrified. The stress was too much and when I kissed you, I forgot for a while. I lost myself. I was out of line." Her heart cracked, and her body made every effort not to clutch each word and take them back, she knew they would hurt him, but better that than for them to keep on like this. The pain of separation was so much worse than what she'd gone through the night before.

He turned his face away and stepped back through the door, closing it enough to hide his face. "I suspected as much."

The door clicked shut behind him and she collapsed for a moment in the chair and let the tears fall freely. Clint was the best thing to happen to her, and now he was gone.

* * *

Despite wanting to turn and run, Clint couldn't do that to Tam. Just like with Mary, he'd let himself have feelings that weren't returned. Would he ever be able to read women?

The truth hurt. He'd known that his whole life. If something was too easy, it probably wasn't right, and they'd come together as easy as biscuits and eggs. She'd seemed to be perfect. More than Mary. When Mary had died, he'd been hurt, so hurt he'd refused to talk about her. Tam left a hole. He'd need a lot of time to heal from this. He focused on waiting for her and watching around him while he said a prayer for healing. The usual peace of prayer didn't fill him this time. Neither did the quiet of the morning. Nothing seemed right or usual.

Clint waited until Tamala emerged from the inn and then locked it behind her, keeping his distance as she wanted, but he couldn't leave her and Mark alone. If anything happened, he'd be there to help. After the short walk back to his office, he indicated she needed to wait for a few minutes in the front with Mark while he spoke to Grainger.

He strode into his office and found Law Enforcement Ranger William Grainger warming his hands by Clint's small office heater. "I don't know how it's possible. The temp is the same in Hot Springs as it is here, but the air sure feels colder." He rubbed his palms together.

"That it does. Must be all the open spaces and wind." Clint peeled off his coat and hung it on the peg near the door. He sat down in the big chair behind his desk, glad that this finally signaled the end. Piles of papers waited for his attention, but most would have to sit longer.

None were more important than getting one poacher out of the park.

William had an easy way about him, like a cowboy who'd been thrown a few times and knew he would be again. Being ready for anything made all the difference. He tugged his phone from inside his vest and glanced at the time. "Is Miss Roth on her way?"

He hated stalling his friend. William had driven all the way from Hot Springs behind a huge plow to get here. He'd expected everything and everyone to be ready for him. "She's in the front office with Mark. She'll come in shortly to tell you everything. I can start with what I know."

"Have you witnessed this, or is it some kind of phantom, attention-seeking behavior? We've never had anything like this happen before. My first instinct is disbelief. A poacher, and not only a poacher, but a man we both know…hunting a *person*?"

He'd worried William wouldn't believe that, especially since Tamala had a healthy dose of skepticism about Grainger's possible participation in the crimes.

"Tamala saw him shoot at one of our bears almost a week ago. I included that part in the report I sent to you. Anders was out, in plain sight. He saw her and it was enough to make him want to silence her. I heard the shot and came to investigate. When I arrived, he was aiming at Tamala. At the time, I didn't realize it was Anders. Over time, we've learned of his convoluted plot to take back his ranger position. I can only assume he's the mastermind behind the rash of bear and bison poaching in the last year, since he knows their habits as well as any of us do." That was speculation, but the numbers had skyrocketed while he was a ranger and never went down after he left.

"I see. That is never going to happen. It isn't widely known, but Anders didn't retire. He was threatened with demotion for his conduct." Grainger sat on the other side of the desk and typed on his phone. He glanced at Clint's desk, asking silent permission to use it.

Clint cleared a space for him and nodded his agreement. "At first, there were three, possibly four of them. But I haven't seen the others in days. They had to have left when we closed everything in the park. They also may have kidnapped a naturalist, Meghan Dale. We've been unable to find any sign of her and her phone has gone to voicemail for days."

"Were all of the accomplices poachers?" He glanced up briefly, then continued typing.

Clint wasn't sure. Tamala probably couldn't tell Grainger either. "We aren't sure. Anders was the only one she witnessed."

He nodded slightly, his fingers flying over the screen. "Jackson, is there anything more you'd like to add?" Though they were friends, this was all business. He had to get this part right or they'd call his job into question.

He gritted his teeth and forced his mind back to the present. "Yes. Tamala is hesitant to talk to you because she was sure someone high in the ranks here at Yellowstone was working with the poachers. When we discovered who he was, and her theory was proven correct…let's just say her trust has been violated.

"Also, his reason for hunting Tamala is that he wants to kill her and believes he can provide evidence that I did it."

"And if you were convicted of murdering a naturalist, his old job would open up. How convenient. Do we now have any idea where he is?"

Not as of that morning. Clint had hoped to walk into this meeting with that exact information, allowing Tamala to relax, because they had all they needed to finish the job.

"I wish I knew. Early this morning, I left Tamala with Mark so I could check all the places we've seen him. He isn't in any of them. I don't know how many hideouts he's had or how he keeps moving. There aren't that many areas in the park available to him. You know as well as I do what's locked and what's not. Though, as a former ranger, he might have keys that he copied while he still worked here."

He considered the heater he'd used at the inn for Tamala. The machine was completely portable, and its use wouldn't be visible. It was expensive, but not for someone who thought he'd be rich soon. They were safe for indoors and didn't make smoke or create much light. All this time he'd been assuming the poacher had used resources available, but he had to have had everything in place, which was how he'd been one step ahead all the time.

Tamala slowly came in, looking nervous. She walked past him and sat in the chair along the wall, away from him and Grainger.

William held out his hand. "Miss Roth, thank you for joining us. Clint and I were discussing the incident when this all started. Why don't you tell me a bit about the situation that led to these events?"

She shot Clint a glance, but he wasn't about to give

in to fear now. He'd said what he needed to without ignoring her concerns.

"He was down by the falls. I'd taken a hike there because I saw Mama 228 there many times. I only saw her that day after the gunshot." Her face crumpled slightly. "At least he missed and she made it to safety."

He wanted to go to her, offer support. Living animals were her passion, especially making sure they lived as long as they could in a wild setting. Seeing what she had had broken her heart and he'd missed that part.

"I see, that's when you saw Anders for the first time?" He stared at her as if he was still thinking she could be lying, and the idea bubbled in Clint's stomach. She told the truth.

"Yes, that's right." She clenched the arms of the chair tightly.

"And how do you think he continues to track you in Yellowstone?"

Clint ached to lay a reassuring hand on her shoulder, to let her know he was right there, and he'd do all he could to make this end for her. But she didn't want his touch. The intimate part of their relationship hadn't been real. No matter how real it was to him.

"We kept moving until we found a place that was secure enough to keep him out for a few days. Then he found us here, too. I've been too busy running for my life to give it much thought." She held out her arms and yanked back her sleeves, showing all the tiny cuts that monster had made over her skin.

"And this happened when?" William didn't miss a beat. He was a ranger, not there to support or show emotion. Only lead.

She closed her eyes and dropped her hands into her lap. "Last night."

"Right before he disappeared again?" William asked as he typed some more.

Clint answered for her. "Correct."

Ranger Grainger tapped his phone and then folded his hands. "It sounds to me like we have a manhunt on our hands. I'd like to put together a few people from your team, Clint, to canvass the area."

Clint wished he could see outside, but he knew without seeing that the weather would be against them; thick dark clouds blocked the light. "At least it's not snowing now. He's had at least twelve hours. We'll need to act fast."

"I volunteer." Tamala raised her hand, then dropped it.

"I think that's a dangerous situation. Clint, you know this part of the park better than anyone. I want Miss Roth in the most secure location you can think of. Somewhere we know this guy won't find her, because I need the help of every man available."

Tamala looked over her shoulder at him, then led the way out without saying a word.

EIGHTEEN

There were a limited number of places to hide Tamala in the park where no one could find her. Clint was one of only a few people who had keys to the Old Faithful Inn, but if her attacker saw her, breaking open a window to get her was easy. If he and the other rangers were off hunting for Anders, he could get to her without interference.

Anders had already been to many of the most likely places: his cabin, hers and his office. If he had access to those, he probably had access anywhere he wanted to go. The visitor's center had been locked up tight, but had banks of windows and no heat. The safety of the engineering staff was too important to ask her to stay with any of them all day, not to mention they were often outside. They were not prepared to take on that task, and he refused to ask them. Their target was too dangerous.

Tamala slowed her steps. "Where are we going?"

Nothing around him gave him any more inspiration, and he forced himself to block all desire to keep her at his side all day like he'd done when they locked up the park. That might solve one problem, but it brought on a whole host of others. She distracted him, which had gotten her injured in the past. He wouldn't take a risk when this was their last shot at success. If the poacher got to Tamala, he was still going to jail either way. The killer had nothing to lose. Distraction diverted his focus and might allow the poacher to get his target.

"I considered the clinic. No windows. Small, to keep in the heat. Only way in is the front door." He shrugged, hoping he sounded like he was talking to anyone other than the woman he was growing to care deeply for. She wanted distant, cordial, cold. If that's what she wanted, he'd oblige, but the task wasn't easy.

Tamala shivered. "I don't like that idea. No one is ever comfortable at the doctor's office. What will I do all day?"

"The nurse has some books in the lobby. We'll move one of the chairs to the exam room, so you'll have somewhere comfortable to sit…"

She interrupted. "Have you ever sat in a clinic chair for more than a few minutes? They aren't comfortable."

She was doing it again. Shutting down his suggestions because she'd already formulated what she wanted to do. "I suppose you have a better idea?"

"I do. I want to stay with you. I hike all day. Maybe not this time of year, but I'm capable. I'll stay around you all day. He might try, but he won't get me if I'm with you."

He couldn't deny that's what he wanted, but he was under a direct order. Grainger was now his superior officer. "If I was the one making the decision, you would be with me. I don't like leaving you anywhere. Do you know how hard this is on me, to lock you behind a door and pray you're still there when I return?" Maybe she really didn't. Maybe he'd just put his heart on his sleeve again. He should know better.

She swallowed hard. "I didn't know." Tamala took a deep breath and glanced around her. "If you think the clinic is the safest place, the most secure, then that's where I'll go. But can I use the computers, at least?"

He hadn't wanted her online before, but now they knew who they were after, there was no reason for her not to be. "If that will make the time pass easier for you, I can log you in without compromising any medical records. You'll be able go online, but not much else."

She gave a weak smile. "That's all I need."

She followed him toward the clinic. He tugged her phone from his pocket and handed it to her. "Mark went back to your place to look for Anders this morning and brought it."

She clutched it to her chest like a long-lost friend. "Please, tell him thank you. I'll charge it in the breakroom when I get there. I'll keep it on me at all times."

He unlocked the door and took her back to one of the windowless exam rooms, moved the most comfortable chair he could find inside, logged into the computer, and then stood there, feeling there was something he should do or say before he left. She waved briefly, like he would see her again in a few hours. Despite his resolve to feel nothing, he dearly hoped that was the case.

"I'll be back for you."

She blushed slightly with a small smile. "I know."

He scanned the area for footprints or any sign of Anders as he headed back to his office. If he drew their guy away from Tamala, that would be the best outcome. He'd lure the killer right into a trap. Unfortunately, nothing moved nearby. Yellowstone was so expansive, sometimes movements went unnoticed with the vast surroundings. After living there for years, he still found it impossible to take in everything.

Once he reached his office, the space was full with three members from his team and Grainger. "Most of you know why we're here. Some don't. This isn't your usual fugitive situation. This guy knows the park well and doesn't care what he has to do to escape."

William turned a small laptop in a bulletproof case to face them and a familiar face appeared. Tamala's attacker mugged for the camera in his olive drab ranger suit and hat. "It took me a while to find a shot of the man's face—he seems to have stayed hidden even when he worked for the park. Anders has made comments about Mama 228 in poaching groups on the dark web." He nodded at Clint. "This is our guy, right?"

Without the irrational flare to his eyes, he looked different, but the image was him. "Correct." Clint crossed his arms and avoided saying the obvious. The guys in the room would know this picture wouldn't do much good for the two guys who hadn't worked under Anders. If they found him, he'd be wearing a huge coat and hat, possibly goggles and ski mask, which he'd rarely removed so far.

"He's most likely on foot since I haven't noted any strange vehicles here," Clint offered.

"Other than the Hummer that you reported?" William seemed to be testing whether he'd filled in his team about all that had happened.

"Correct, though there was nothing inside that made

seizing the vehicle necessary. He'll have resources since he knows what to expect from the winter, as he lived here for fifteen years. The Hummer must have had supplies when they came into Yellowstone. We've found an abandoned tent, wrappers, a pull sled; he's used skis and he's been moving pretty freely around the park without notice."

That galled him the most. Anders acted so naturally in his environment no one had questioned why he was there. "He's also possibly diabetic, so wherever you find him will have to be somewhere to keep food or insulin cold but not frozen."

Grainger leaned against the desk. "That's easy since he's an outdoorsman. Freezer packs can be left outside to freeze, then rotated to keep a cooler at refrigerator temp. Insulin is small. A handheld cooler is enough, and he could live off protein bars. People with motive and extreme desire can survive in the worst conditions. But I'll grant you, it's not exact and I'm surprised he's not pretty sick by now."

He knew all that, but he'd assumed a poacher wouldn't, but a ranger would. "Tamala and I have encountered him a few times. Directly after we see him, he's moved. I think he has a few comfortable locations, which means he's probably running out of hiding spots, just like we were."

Mark nodded. "We went through last night and sealed the bungalows to make sure no one entered where they shouldn't. We don't normally, but in this case, we thought it was a good idea."

"I agree." William tore off a promotional map of Yellowstone from Clint's desk. "Mark where you sealed them. Clint, mark where he's been. Maybe we'll see a pattern."

One thing he wouldn't do is tell anyone but Grainger where Tamala hid for the day. He trusted his team, but the walls seemed to have ears and he wouldn't lead anyone to her door.

Once they'd marked up the map, William gave them each a blocked area to hunt and turned them loose. Since there was an odd number of people, he went alone. The only partner he'd wanted to work with was in hiding.

Tamala set the small space heater used for ice fishing under her desk to warm her feet, then settled into the office chair at the desk. She'd barricaded the door, plugged in her charger for her phone so she'd have it if she needed it, and pushed the chair Clint had brought into the room against the door, leaving only a very narrow strip of light along the bottom.

At least for now, she was alone. Her breath stalled in her throat as she sighed. This park had been home for the better part of three years. Now the comfy safe feeling had left. *He'd* been here. She'd hidden to save her life here. Would her beloved Yellowstone ever feel welcoming again?

With the few hours she and Clint had lived in his office, she hadn't allowed herself to really think about what had happened. Where might their relationship go from here? Where was Meghan and was she connected to all of this, or had she been kidnapped? What would life look like on the other side of this mess?

She shook the thoughts from her mind and tried to focus, but every subtle bump of the snow sliding off the roof or creak of the old building made her jump. At least Clint was doing something active. She was waiting to be found.

No matter how much she searched online, the task wasn't enough to distract her. Her mind kept wandering to Clint and what he was doing. Was he in danger? Did he need her help, or had he finally given up on her as it seemed he had?

If she was out there helping, she wouldn't be bored, nor lonely. A moving target was more difficult to locate. She headed for the door and stopped the moment her hand touched the chair in the way. The last time she'd thought about going off on her own, she'd ended up needing rescue. Because of that, she hadn't considered it again, and wouldn't.

She should've listened to Clint. Now Clint was out there alone. Even on a team, the poacher won every time. No matter what they tried, they barely escaped.

She paced until the room was so dim she had to turn on the light. After checking her phone, she found no word from Clint. Either he'd forgotten to come get her or something had gone wrong. They wouldn't keep searching in the dark, would they? Anders was always more active at night.

A notification lit up the screen of her phone and she winced at the three-digit number of missed emails. That would distract her for a few minutes, though most of what she received was garbage; she was still waiting for the park service to approve her request to stay year-round to study.

She pressed open the email app and stared at the bright screen. Would Clint want her to stay there all night? Her gaze flicked to the clock and it was well past dark. Part of her knew she had to trust him, but he also had to trust *her*. The bridge had to go both ways.

Not that trust mattered now. She'd uttered the words no relationship ever healed from. "I didn't mean it when we kissed…"

Her chest ached as she felt the loneliness that would be hers for a lifetime. She had no other close friends, only acquaintances. No one to share her worries with. No one to help her. No one to trust. Except Clint, and she'd shut the door in his face.

NINETEEN

Tamala slowly checked her phone email but the more time she took, the more antsy she became. Where was Clint? At the bottom of her stack of emails, a notification from her personal email account stopped her cold. The subject read: Tamala, I need you to read this right away. No one ever emailed her there, but this didn't look like spam.

This is Meghan. I'm so sorry. Some men got to me the day after I spoke to you. I broke into their computers, and I'll be deleting this right after I send. Please give everything to the authorities so they can get me out of here.

Meghan had been kidnapped, not left. Clint had hinted she might be one of them, but poor Meghan had only been in the wrong place at the wrong time. She prayed they would take the poacher alive so he could lead them to her. She signed back in to the main computer to download the file attached to the email. She'd hoped to avoid signing in to her email on a public computer, but this was too important not to.

The attachment was a large one and she wasn't sure what she'd see when she opened it. Was this a tracking link? Meghan might have said she was kidnapped to get her to open the file, but what if she wasn't? She held her breath and clicked on the file.

A map of Yellowstone appeared on her screen. There were red marks over her cabin and the other places the poacher had taken her, except one. Even the place where they'd found the tent had a mark.

She flipped the map the proper direction to get a better view. The one spot she hadn't been lately was a little cabin very close to Old Faithful. From that cabin, the geothermal feature would be practically in his backyard. But did that mean he was hiding there? He'd been run out of all the other spots. Yellowstone was huge. If the search team had fanned out from Clint's office, they would've found the poacher right away.

They hadn't looked in those cabins because they were in plain sight and, being owned by the concessioners, the LE team didn't have a key. Anders always hid out in the open, tempting them to find him.

He could've easily been watching Clint take her to the clinic with a pair of binoculars. He probably had watched them just that way, since he'd caught them so many times. Those cabins were the perfect hideout and probably where he'd spent most of his time. Why bring her to his secret place when he had so many satellite locations at his disposal?

She shivered at the realization that the night they'd spent in the cabin, they'd been mere yards away from him. The car had probably picked him up and taken him to a few cabins around where they'd gone. Had the poacher known, they would be dead.

"I have to tell…" She stopped and closed her eyes. Who would she tell? Clint? He was of course the first to her mind. If she told Grainger, he'd want to know how she got the information. He might find it suspicious that she wasn't near anyone all day, but suddenly had incriminating evidence. Did she believe what Meghan said about being kidnapped?

She had no one else. She had to tell Clint and she had to come clean with him about how she really felt. Going through this alone was too terrifying. She scrolled to the bottom to make sure there wasn't anything else on the copy. If she hadn't rotated the image vertically instead of landscape view, she'd have missed it. In red pen, the person who'd scanned the map had written, *I wrote this out so you'd know where to find him. Hope it's useful.*

She hit Print and rushed to put her coat and boots back on. Clint had to return any minute or she'd take her chances and go find him. Bear spray in one pocket, the map in the other, she reached for her phone to tell Clint. The poacher didn't know it, but his number was up.

Clint's calves and thighs hurt from trudging through the deep snow. He was freezing cold and starving. His hunting area had led to nothing, and from what he heard on the walkies, no one else had better luck. He needed to check with them in person, then go check on Tam like he'd promised.

He plodded back toward his office, wishing for the first time that Yellowstone offered fast food. He'd still have to make supper when he got back to the office and probably eat alone. William would probably want Tamala to stay in the secure location.

He clenched his fist and forced himself to pay attention to his surroundings. Just because he hadn't seen a single hint of anything that day didn't mean he wouldn't now. If Anders was hiding, he had the advantage. He could stay where he was and watch Clint.

As he made his way back, his gaze caught on the bungalow Mary had stayed in years before, at least until they'd married. He hadn't intentionally avoided it all this time, but subconsciously he did. Even now, when searching everything mattered most, he'd skipped that one like it didn't exist because of all the memories there.

Tamala deserved better. He slowly made his way to the little brown building that looked like all the others and instead of doing the preliminary check like he had at every other place, he took out the key and shoved the door open.

The house was neat and completely empty of anything but the most basic furniture. The mattress leaned against the wall without bedding, and the few other bits of furniture were empty and clear. Nothing there. Not even memories of Mary. Somewhere along the way, the sting had become less sharp than he'd thought it would be. Losing her had been hard, but the years between made his heart ready for someone new.

He could fix the rift between him and Tam, if he wanted to. If she let him. He locked the door and scanned the sky. Stars dotted the dark expanse above, so clear and bright without all the city lights to dim them. The brilliant snow glistening in the moonlight wasn't enough to blot out the show.

He rushed toward the Old Faithful Inn and found most of the search team there waiting for him outside. "Anyone else find anything?" He wanted to get to Tamala fast. She had to be worried and he wouldn't feel right until he knew she was safe.

The defeated and cold team all shook their heads with a few mumbles. Grainger came around the building. "Nothing with us either. We'll have to rest and start a new search in the morning. Is it possible he's moved to one of the remote cabins?"

Only the strongest, fittest rangers lived in those. None of those rangers would willingly take in someone who shouldn't be there, even someone they knew.

"I can't see him surviving the trek out to one of them in this weather." The snow had let up for a whole day now, but the paths were buried in feet of snow.

"Then he's here unless he left the park. We'll regroup tomorrow."

"Mark has a spare bunk in his barracks." Clint had to find housing for William, and there wasn't an extra couch in the ranger station.

Mark motioned for Grainger to follow him and the group broke up to head for home. Clint rushed for the clinic, praying she'd just waited for him and thankful Grainger hadn't ordered him to keep her there. He'd covered his tracks over when he'd left that morning and the snow was still clear. No one else had entered through the front door.

He unlocked the main door, then headed back for the interior office. After a quick knock, he heard the chair slide to the side, and the door opened. She stood there in her coat, ready for him with the most thankful and open look in her eyes.

"What are you doing? Were you going out?" He hoped not.

"No, I was waiting for you. I was going to call you, but then wanted to speak to you face-to-face. I got word from Meghan." She yanked a paper from her pocket. "That's his location. I know it."

He scanned the sheet. She grabbed a pen off the desk and circled one of the marked cabins. He wasn't sure what to say. "One of our men checked here this afternoon." Though not all the teams had keys to physically check. They'd looked for tracks and signs.

"I know he's there. Do you trust me?"

The words echoed what he'd been thinking about before he'd come. He had to trust her so she could trust him, maybe then what he felt would grow inside her, too. "I do. What do you want to do?"

She smiled and stepped closer, wrapping her arms around his neck. "First, I want to say I'm sorry. I said some things that weren't true. I told you I kissed you because of stress. That was a lie. I realized today that our differences aren't enough to throw away what I think we've got."

He held her closer. "Apology accepted and I'm sorry, too, for holding you back because rejection hurts. I think you're right." He'd been thinking about her all day, despite his promise to himself that he wouldn't. She was going to be on his mind forever, and there wasn't a thing he wanted to change about that.

She stood on her tiptoes and her kiss stole every thought from his mind. He held her close and cupped her face. "I'd stay here with you, but I think we should get this to Grainger right away."

She nodded, her eyes bright. "I don't want to face him in the dark again. Let's call Grainger. That way he can have a plan ready for morning."

"Now, that's a plan we can agree on."

TWENTY

Tamala walked alongside Clint on the way to his office. They'd stayed in the clinic waiting room that night on uncomfortable sofas with the door barricaded. Every noise had sent her heart racing.

Clint tramped the snow in front of her, making a clear path. "Grainger outranks me, but I want you by my side today."

"I'm frightened. I'll admit it. But I'd rather be frightened next to you than wondering where you are. Especially knowing, if he was in that cabin, he could see me at any place you chose to hide me. But, he'll be dangerous when he's cornered." Like a bear. She had to believe today would be the end. She shivered though the temps had warmed to an unseasonable forty degrees. "I'll have something to be very thankful for at Thanksgiving this year."

Clint smiled at her. "I have family in Cody. You're welcome to join us for the holiday. Giving you even more to be thankful for."

Her steps slowed slightly at the thought. She'd never been invited to meet a guy's family. A big step considering they hadn't even been on a date. What if... She refused to ruin anything before it started. "Let's talk about that after today." She refused to think about possibilities until they both survived to tomorrow.

Once they got to his office, most of the team was already there waiting. Clint pulled the map from his pocket. "I informed Grainger last night, but Tamala has been given some inside information that I think will lead us right to our guy." Clint made eye contact with Grainger and she knew he'd given Grainger Meghan's information in private. Hopefully, they'd get her out.

LE Ranger Grainger narrowed his eyes at her but took the paper from Clint and scanned it with an intense stare. He squinted and read the bottom. "This is from our missing person. She's taken a huge risk to get this information to us. Let's not waste it. The minute we're done here, I'll be joining the team that's hunting for her."

Tamala quietly said a prayer for Meghan and her two grown sons who had to be terrified right now. Her gut said Meghan wasn't a willing participant, but a week was a long time to be missing and still be found alive.

She took in a deep breath. "I firmly believe you'll find him there. Probably not for long though. We haven't seen him in over twenty-four hours now. He's been very active lately and might know you're here." She stepped back, out of the ring of men.

Grainger scanned the room. "Pair up with the teams you had yesterday. Hopefully, we'll have him in custody within the hour. If he isn't at this location, we'll have to spread our net farther."

"I'm taking Tamala with me." Clint used his ranger voice and warmth spread through her chest.

"Let it go on record that I don't like this idea." Grainger glanced out the window. "You are the two main targets. If she's coming out into the field, then we'll go as a team of three." He sent his original partner with another team to cover exit points.

He nodded and turned to talk to the other men in the room. Clint held the door for her as they went back out into the cold. "I really want you to say safe today." He waited near the exit for Grainger to join them.

After a moment, he unclipped his walkie from his belt and handed it to her. "Keep this with you. Just in case we get separated. You may not be able to talk but you know what to do. Stay put, I'll be there as fast as humanly possible. I'll find you."

She took the walkie and clipped it to her back pocket, hidden under her borrowed coat. "I have my cell phone, too. If this is too loud, I'll text you."

He frowned and scrubbed his face as he kept his gaze moving, always watching. "Your point is valid. Bringing you along puts you in implicit danger. We can't predict what he'll do when we corner him. I'm torn. I have to help Grainger. I hate to risk not being able to hear you. But I want you with me."

He might be right. The poacher had to be aware today was his last stand and likely he wouldn't make it out of the park a free man. His only way of escape was to act fast and find an off-road exit. He'd been too quiet for too many hours for that not to be the case. There had been nothing on the map about his exit strategy. Which meant they had to act before anyone else arrived to extract him.

"Hopefully, we'll have him in custody soon." He

laughed, but it was humorless. "I mean it, Tam. I want to know the second you feel off. Listen to your instincts. They're good."

His reassurance soothed her frayed nerves. "I will. I'll stay close to you and the walkie. If I feel anything at all, you'll be the first to know."

He headed in front of her through the snow. Tamala wasn't sure how to act, so she followed William and Clint's lead and said nothing. One walked in front, one behind as they headed for the cabin on the map.

Grainger gave her a cursory nod. "I'll go in the cabin first. Clint, you back me if he draws on me. Tamala, you stick to the outer wall and don't let him know you're there."

Clint gave her a reassuring nod. "If he pulls his gun, I'm ready." Or, as ready as he could ever be in that kind of situation. He tried to imagine the bust going completely orderly and to plan. Knock and done. None of this shooting and hiding business that was fit for a movie. There had been enough of that in his park to last a lifetime.

They reached the small cabin within a few minutes. A few sets of footprints outside were solid evidence someone had been there.

"No one is supposed to be here. They are trespassing—you would agree?" He leaned so the body camera on his vest would hear him.

Clint nodded, not sure what the ranger was getting at. "Agreed."

"Good, then I don't need to knock." He checked the knob, and it turned easily.

Clint stepped back and held his breath, gun in hand, leading him. If *he* were hiding from the police, he wouldn't leave his hideout unlocked for anyone to walk in.

Grainger raised his gun and led the way inside. A few seconds later he called, "All clear. Looks like he was here, but he's not now. There's bedding, wrappers, waste. Someone was squatting here."

Clint stepped inside and found a few empty vials of what looked like insulin. There were meal replacement bars and the long knife with a curved point like the one Tamala had described to him. Blankets lay in a wad in the middle of the mattress and a kerosene heater sat on the table right next to it.

"If he's not here, where is he? No one has seen this guy in a day and a half." William holstered his gun.

A shot came from the direction of the inn and Tamala rushed over. Since Anders wasn't in the cabin, he could be anywhere—it would be safer than being outside alone.

Clint grabbed her hand as the three of them silently raced for the inn. When this had been a search mission, she'd wanted to be there. But now she understood why William had wanted her locked away again. A search mission could turn into a defensive procedure.

The snow hadn't slowed the poacher down. Nothing had. She reached the door of the inn at Clint's side as more shots came from inside. Mark lay on the ground with a wound to his side. Grainger knelt over him and took his vitals when Clint blocked her with his body. She wasn't sure if it was protection from Anders or from seeing Mark so injured, but she appreciated it.

"He's alive, but he'll need a whirlybird."

"I'm on it." Clint radioed in for a copter. He finished the transmission then focused on Grainger. "Dave was here, too. They were a team."

Grainger nodded. "We've got to go in, which is the absolute last place I want to take Tamala. She shouldn't be here. She should've stayed where she was yesterday."

"I want to see this end and you can't take the time to find me a safe place now. Go, you have to get Dave out of there," she said.

They followed Grainger inside, Clint still holding tight to her hand. He closed the door behind him and immediately an icy dread stole over her. The inn had always felt comfortable and homey, but now it was as eerie as an abandoned theme park. Rich, warm memories hid just out of reach, steeped in shadow.

She strode in further, near the large fireplace, and a chill wind blew down the chimney. In the dim light, all the rocks of the masonry were dull gray. She turned, feeling the hair on the back of her neck prickle to life.

"He's here," she whispered. Clint had wanted to know. She stuffed her gloves in her pocket to keep her phone at the ready to reach Clint if they got separated. Her heart hammered a warning that she needed to look in every corner.

A door slammed shut down the hall. Grainger took off in pursuit. Clint headed after him, but hesitated. "This feels like a trap."

"Clint, I need room on that bird for two. Dave is down."

Anders appeared from a separate hallway. "How astute of you, Clint."

* * *

Clint's mind raced. He needed to protect Tamala, call in the adjusted order to save his friend's life and stay alive to arrest Anders. How had he gotten inside the inn if Mark and Dave had used his key and locked it behind them?

The other ranger that had been on Mark and Dave's team was still missing, too. What else would they find upstairs? He thanked God they'd only heard two shots so far. Maybe the assistant ranger was still somewhere inside.

He shifted his weight to make sure Tamala was behind him. Above him, an intricate network of wood joists created a solid framework for the interior of the massive structure. Within those areas, hundreds of places for the missing ranger to be.

"I'm smart enough to know that I won't get my position back now," Anders practically snarled.

"Then why are you here?" Clint hoped the sound of his voice would carry to Grainger who could then come and even the odds against them.

"I've so easily taken care of all your men. When I was ranger here, nothing like this would've happened."

Clint let the insult slide off him. "Except you were doing these same things when you held the title. You fired anyone who questioned you." Tamala gripped his waist tightly and he was thankful for her presence behind him, but if Anders shot with his high-powered rifle, they'd both be gone in a heartbeat.

Clint didn't have anything to protect him from a bullet, and his backup was still making sure Dave survived the day. Mark still waited outside, alone, for the chopper.

He stepped out of the shadows, holding his hands up, showing his pistol. "We trade. You let her go and take me instead."

Anders threw back his head and laughed. "That's not how this works. You've both seen my face, and you're as good as dead anyway." He raised his handgun level with Clint's chest. "I wanted to have so much more fun, but there's no time now."

Clint tackled Tamala to the floor moments before he heard the blast of the gun. Tamala covered her head, and he searched the nearest hallway for a place to duck and hide. He had to protect her at all costs.

"That wasn't very sporting of you, Clint. Maybe you don't know how this works, being on national soil too much. You probably don't hunt, do you?" Anders's slow footfalls came closer. "I put your skull in my sights…"

Tamala clung to Clint as he maneuvered them down the hall.

"Clint! Report!" Grainger yelled from the distant room. "Clint?"

"Suspect in sight." Clint sounded far too calm while Tamala's heart raced. She never wanted to be in a situation like this again.

Anders appeared at the entrance to the hall and Clint shoved her into an open room as he raised his pistol. A shot rang out and Clint dropped like a rock. A scream tore from Tamala's throat. He'd protected her instead of himself…

If Clint was still alive, he wouldn't be for long. She had to get his gun. "Grainger! Clint is down. Help!"

She peered out into the hallway just as Grainger leveled his gun from the end of the hall. The sight of Clint in Anders's crosshairs sickened her to her core.

Anders glanced up at her for a moment with cold, dark eyes, then leveled the gun at her.

TWENTY-ONE

In the span of a second, Tamala's life flashed, mimicking the burst of the chamber fire. All her decisions had been safe. All her life had been behind a desk or in the shadows. Even tracking the bears had been safe because she'd remained hidden while she did it.

Take chances, her soul prodded. She flung herself over Clint as the poacher raised his gun toward her, surprise slackening his jaw.

Blood seeped from Clint's shoulder, but the poacher hadn't looked closely at Clint yet and she wouldn't turn his attention back to finish the job. Tamala curled her body, protecting Clint from another shot.

Anders cursed as Grainger leaned further into the hall.

His hand seemed to move in slow motion as Anders gripped her arm and sent her flying back into the opposite wall. Her head cracked against the hard wood and a bright light flashed before her eyes. Through blurry vision, she watched as he slowly crouched for Clint's gun. There was no way to stop him. Her limbs wouldn't respond.

He rose to stand and aimed the pistol at her. At that

range, she wouldn't survive. Her mind knew as much. His laugh echoed off the walls as he lifted the gun until she could see the gaping end of the barrel. Her brain wouldn't clear, no matter how hard she blinked and focused on getting up to escape.

Clint lay a few feet away and, she saw him flex his fingers and reach for her. "No!" She found her voice.

A gunshot exploded behind her, filling her head with light and sound. Then silence. She opened her eyes as someone pressed her neck, checking her pulse.

"I've got three injured on the second floor of the Old Faithful Inn, and one just outside the front door. I need rescue ambulances. Stat. Three gunshot wounds, two likely concussions, one for a bag." Grainger's voice was steady and calm.

A bag? She made her way to her knees and found Clint still lying where he'd been, still staring at her. His eyes letting her know he was very much alive. Grainger crouched a few feet from her, talking into his walkie. Though Anders's eyes were open, they didn't move, didn't blink, didn't look evil anymore.

It was over. At least for now. Until his team learned he hadn't been successful in silencing her. The short-lived peace was all it took for the tears she'd held back to finally release. Her body finally listened to her command, and she crawled to Clint's side.

"What can I do?" she whispered.

He reached out for her. "Stay here. Grainger says help is on the way." His voice was ragged, soft.

She gripped his hand and pulled her gloves from her pocket to use as a pillow for him.

"I'm sorry, Tam. Shouldn't've let you come with."

She brushed his damp hair from his face. "You listened to your intuition. I agreed with you. He followed the search team in here and came in after Mark."

Grainger came over to Clint and checked the wound. "I've got my first aid kit in my car. It's not going to do much, but the birds are on the way as fast as they can be. Hold tight." He rushed off to get it.

"Clint, just because I want to give you a reason to fight. I want you to know, I love you. I fought those feelings for the last few days, but I'm pretty sure I've loved you from the start."

He nodded with a pained chuckle. "I didn't want to admit what I felt either, but I love you, too. This won't stop me. Hurts more than I thought possible, but this isn't the end of me."

She leaned down and kissed his forehead. His skin was so hot and damp from the pain. "I hope they get here fast. The snow stopped, so the copter shouldn't have trouble. I'm praying."

"Praying is a good place to start." He closed his eyes and squeezed her hand.

Without Grainger between her and her attacker, she examined Anders. Something had switched in his brain. Pride, jealousy and revenge had made him choose the wrong path. Before he'd come after her, he'd been no more important than anyone else who hunted animals illegally. He'd done nothing to earn a death sentence.

Now he wouldn't get the chance to ever make his poor choices right. She wanted to be thankful that he would never chase her again but seeing the end of someone's life left no room for thankfulness. Only regret. Like Clint said, the kind she couldn't change.

Mr. Henderson called from the entrance to the hall. "Grainger says we're not allowed down there because it's a crime scene. Are you all right? Need anything I can send up with the ranger until the life flight gets here?"

Clint was sweating, but only because of his injury. He'd shiver if he went into shock, and the temperature was freezing cold. "Blankets, please," she called back. "Thank you!"

Within a half hour, Clint lay on a stretcher headed for the whirlybird. She rode along, but not as a patient. No one was going to separate them now.

EPILOGUE

Thanksgiving Day

Clint's parents' dog Boomer the Pomeranian met him at the door, barking and talking as she raced around his feet. Tamala gasped at his side and gripped his arm. She'd been careful to only ever walk on his left side since he'd been released from the hospital and he was thankful for her sensitivity.

"She won't hurt you."

"Oh, I know. I love dogs." Tamala got down on her knees and held out her hand for the little orange ball of fluff.

Boomer sniffed and yipped, flinging herself in Tamala's lap. Clint laughed as Tamala squealed with glee. He hadn't heard her so happy since they'd met. He hoped the gift nestled in his backpack would make her even happier.

His parents rushed down the hall and helped Tamala off the floor, then gave her hugs. She'd gotten close to them when he'd been recuperating from his gunshot wound. Now he only had to distract her for a few months while they waited for the rest of the poaching group to make it to court. Then they could move on with normal life.

"Clint, you're looking well. Tamala must be taking good care of you." Mom eyed him.

He'd gotten unique permission for Tamala to stay on-site until mid-March when the park reopened for the spring season. The park service hadn't wanted to do it, but one of the women engineers took her in. He'd been glad for at least one winter season with Tam, even if this was the only one. She'd said she liked to study her research during the winter and he could give her that time if she still wanted it.

"She's doing great. I might be back to regular work faster than expected." He laughed at her immediately guarded look like he should behave himself.

"I don't think you should push yourself too fast. Let the park give you the time you deserve to heal," Tamala said.

He'd love to take more time, but he was a law enforcement ranger and the Old Faithful section needed him. But her worry meant she cared. "I'll rest as long as I can stand to."

Tam rolled her eyes and picked up Boomer. "Which is about as long as your dog will stand being held." Boomer immediately wagged her tail hard enough to wiggle right out of Tam's arms.

Everyone laughed as the waggling dog raced around. This was home. The feeling was exactly what he'd always wanted, everything he'd thought he'd lost when Mary died. But nothing met his hopes like Tam did.

"Did you get a response back on your grant request?" Mom asked Tam.

He hadn't heard anything about a grant, and he felt

every muscle tense until the pain in his shoulder forced him to let his fear go.

Tam smiled at him. "I hadn't mentioned anything to Clint yet. The grant was supposed to be a surprise. I didn't want to say anything and worry him if I got rejected." She turned to him. "I've applied for a grant to work in the park researching how or if certain aspects of the climate affect the geysers. I haven't heard back yet."

He stared at her for a moment, gathering the right words to say. "Would this be in addition to what you do in Yellowstone? Your team would miss you as a naturalist if it did." But the research was valuable, and he'd still see her. Just not every day as he had before.

"This would be in addition to. I might also be able to stay during the off-season with approval. Since it's for research."

"What about all your bear research?"

She smiled at him and slipped her hand into his. "I will always be fascinated by bears and keeping them safe. Maybe someday I'll return to what interested me before when I feel more comfortable hiking alone again. But for now, I don't want to put myself in the way of danger until I know I've got help and resources to back me up. At the very least, I need to find someone willing to partner with me."

He'd said the same thing to her in an attempt to give her reasons to stay. He hadn't been quiet about keeping his real feelings out of those reasons. Sending her back out into dangerous territory, with no one and no documentation, often in the evening, seemed like the epitome of dangerous. It was a wonder she hadn't been injured before. And if all went to plan, she'd have someone she could rely on to go with her, namely him.

"Good," Dad agreed before Clint had a chance. "We love having you close."

Mom tugged her into another hug, then gestured for the kitchen. "We should all go sit down before Boomer realizes the table has been set."

Everyone laughed and as Dad and Mom headed to the dining room, Clint caught Tamala's arm, stalling her momentarily. "Thanks for telling me."

She blushed slightly. "I'm sorry I didn't tell you sooner. I wasn't hiding it. I didn't want to get your hopes up if I got turned down."

"I understand." He had met with Grainger and talked briefly to him about the case. Talking about it at the supper table just didn't seem right. "Grainger called me this morning. The other men were caught, but Meghan wasn't with them. They wouldn't talk about her and acted as if they didn't know her."

Tamala's forehead rippled in confusion. "I haven't heard from her since, but maybe she's gone into hiding... I hope." She bit her lip.

He could see the memories creeping back into her thoughts of all they'd been through. "Grainger said they had a dog do a search there with some of her clothing left behind. She was with them. They found her in a ravine about three miles from the hideout." He knew Tam would be hurt, but would want to know.

"Thank you for telling me. I'd heard they'd been arrested and hadn't heard anything about her."

"Grainger has a friend from the FBI looking into it. He doesn't think she was guilty, but it doesn't matter much now. I'm sorry."

She brushed her hair behind her ears. "I'm sorry

she's gone. I was so worried she was a part of the poaching ring, especially with the way she acted that first day after the attack." She bit her lip. "I don't want to think about it now. This is Thanksgiving. Let's be thankful."

He couldn't agree more. Carefully, he slung his backpack off his shoulder and unzipped the top with one hand. "I have something for you before we go in to eat."

He said a little prayer before pulling a small bear stuffy from his bag and handing it to her. "To replace the one he stole. I know you don't ever want the other one back."

"Oh!" She cried and hugged the bear to her cheek, then pulled it away with a confused look. "It's...cold around the neck." She ran her finger around it.

He laughed as he lowered to one knee and took the bear back. The ring was attached to a ribbon around its neck like a collar. He slipped the band off and offered it to her. "I have to admit you stole my heart, Tam. Will you marry me?"

She landed on her knees in front of him and hugged him tight. He didn't care about the sharp pain through his shoulder; he just wanted an answer. She released him and slid the band on her finger.

"Before I met you, I never thought... Never." A tear ran down her cheek. "Are you sure?"

He laughed, confused by the question. Of course, he was sure. Nothing was more real to him than what he felt for Tamala. "Absolutely."

"Then yes. One hundred times, yes!"

* * * * *

*Find strength and determination in stories
of faith and love in the face of danger.*

*Look for six new releases every month,
available wherever Love Inspired Suspense
books and ebooks are sold.*

Find more great reads at www.LoveInspired.com

Dear Reader,

Thank you for joining me on this harrowing trip through Yellowstone in my first Love Inspired Suspense novel. I loved doing the research for this book so much that visiting Yellowstone is now on my bucket list.

I have a few friends who live around Yellowstone and talk about it all the time. It's truly more wonderful than I can describe. The book itself came to be when my friend was telling me about a bear who is very popular in Wyoming, she is known as "the Queen," bear 339. She will be twenty-seven years old by the time this is printed and is a really amazing bear. In the spring of 2022, she emerged from torpor (semi-hibernation) with her four cubs in tow. If you've never heard of her, be sure to look her up. She's had a pretty amazing life.

From the moment I started reading about her, a story formed in my head of a devoted naturalist, willing to risk her life to make sure a beloved bear continued to live on in the wild. The rest is history. I hope you join me in the future for more adventure! You can find my other books at www.KariTrumbo.com.

Blessings,
Kari

Get 3 FREE REWARDS!

We'll send you 2 FREE Books plus a FREE Mystery Gift.

FREE Value Over **$20**

Both the **Love Inspired®** and **Love Inspired® Suspense** series feature compelling novels filled with inspirational romance, faith, forgiveness and hope.

YES! Please send me 2 FREE novels from the Love Inspired or Love Inspired Suspense series and my FREE gift (gift is worth about $10 retail). After receiving them, if I don't wish to receive any more books, I can return the shipping statement marked "cancel." If I don't cancel, I will receive 6 brand-new Love Inspired Larger-Print books or Love Inspired Suspense Larger-Print books every month and be billed just $6.49 each in the U.S. or $6.74 each in Canada. That is a savings of at least 16% off the cover price. It's quite a bargain! Shipping and handling is just 50¢ per book in the U.S. and $1.25 per book in Canada.* I understand that accepting the 2 free books and gift places me under no obligation to buy anything. I can always return a shipment and cancel at any time by calling the number below. The free books and gift are mine to keep no matter what I decide.

Choose one: ☐ **Love Inspired Larger-Print** (122/322 BPA GRPA)   ☐ **Love Inspired Suspense Larger-Print** (107/307 BPA GRPA)   ☐ **Or Try Both!** (122/322 & 107/307 BPA GRRP)

Name (please print)

Address   Apt. #

City   State/Province   Zip/Postal Code

Email: Please check this box ☐ if you would like to receive newsletters and promotional emails from Harlequin Enterprises ULC and its affiliates. You can unsubscribe anytime.

Mail to the Harlequin Reader Service:
IN U.S.A.: P.O. Box 1341, Buffalo, NY 14240-8531
IN CANADA: P.O. Box 603, Fort Erie, Ontario L2A 5X3

Want to try 2 free books from another series? Call 1-800-873-8635 or visit www.ReaderService.com.

*Terms and prices subject to change without notice. Prices do not include sales taxes, which will be charged (if applicable) based on your state or country of residence. Canadian residents will be charged applicable taxes. Offer not valid in Quebec. This offer is limited to one order per household. Books received may not be as shown. Not valid for current subscribers to the Love Inspired or Love Inspired Suspense series. All orders subject to approval. Credit or debit balances in a customer's account(s) may be offset by any other outstanding balance owed by or to the customer. Please allow 4 to 6 weeks for delivery. Offer available while quantities last.

Your Privacy—Your information is being collected by Harlequin Enterprises ULC, operating as Harlequin Reader Service. For a complete summary of the information we collect, how we use this information and to whom it is disclosed, please visit our privacy notice located at corporate.harlequin.com/privacy-notice. From time to time we may also exchange your personal information with reputable third parties. If you wish to opt out of this sharing of your personal information, please visit readerservice.com/consumerschoice or call 1-800-873-8635. **Notice to California Residents**—Under California law, you have specific rights to control and access your data. For more information on these rights and how to exercise them, visit corporate.harlequin.com/california-privacy.

LIRLIS23

HARLEQUIN
PLUS

Try the best multimedia subscription service for romance readers like you!

Read, Watch and Play.

Experience the easiest way to get the romance content you crave.

Start your **FREE TRIAL** at
www.harlequinplus.com/freetrial.